Elizabeth Bennett

NEW ENGLISH LIBRARY

A New English Library Original Publication, 1984

First NEL Paperback Edition April 1984

NEL Books are published by
New English Library,
Mill Road, Dunton Green,
Sevenoaks, Kent.
Editorial office: 47 Bedford Square, London WC1B 3DP

Typeset by Fleet Graphics, Enfield, Middlesex

Printed in Great Britain by
Hunt Barnard Printing Ltd., Aylesbury, Bucks.

British Library C.I.P.

Bennett, Elizabeth
Even chance.
I. Title
823'.914[F] PR6052.E5/

ISBN 0-450-05058-0

To my kind and patient friends,
Lena and Cathy,
to whom nothing like this happened either.

CHAPTER ONE

THE VILLA, which was perched on the mountainside above the little village of Kritia on the north coast of Crete, was painted pale blue. It was a new building, and the woodwork —the doors and window-frames and shutters—was of natural wood varnished to the colour and shine of Cretan honey, and the pantiles on the roof were of thick, curving terracotta and looked strangely as if they had been made of Plasticine.

At one o'clock, when the heat was at its greatest and the spring sunshine fell clear and sparkling like a bar of crystal from the cornflower-blue arch of the sky, the working day at the villa came to an end, and Jennie Savage and her husband Miles Egerton emerged on to the veranda from doors at opposite ends. Jennie stretched luxuriantly and went to lean on the rail and look down at the sea that crawled lazily a hundred feet below at the end of an almost sheer drop.

'Such a colour!' she said. 'It never ceases to amaze me that anything in the world could be so blue as the Aegean.'

'So you never cease to remark,' Miles said, flopping down on to a chair. Jennie turned her head to look at him as he scraped the chair irritably backwards into the strip of shadow along the back of the veranda.

'Book not going well?' she enquired gently.

'Why should you think that?' he asked suspiciously.

'Just the absence of your usual sunny good humour,' Jennie said.

The irony was not lost on Miles. He put his hands behind his head and stared up at the sky and said, 'Living with a parrot would spoil anyone's temper. You make the same remark every day.'

'It's true every day,' said Jennie, turning away again.

'That doesn't make it any more worth hearing,' Miles snapped.

'Don't listen then,' she retorted.

'Oh, that's a useful suggestion. Do you recommend earplugs?'

Jennie didn't answer, and they remained in silence for a few minutes, a silence unbroken until the arrival of Sofia bearing a tray on which were two glasses and a tall glass jug in which ice cubes clinked evocatively.

'Kalimeras tas,' she said cheerfully, and Jennie smiled a greeting and came to draw the table into position for Sofia to put down the tray. Miles neither spoke nor moved, but remained staring up at the sky. Sofia and Jennie exchanged a glance. He would be better when he'd had his first drink of the day, they both thought. Sofia was fat and elderly with a gnarled brown face and she rolled as she walked on her broken-down black shoes. She wore a black dress and black cardigan even through the most appalling heat, but as a gesture of anglicisation to her employers she wore her head uncovered. She and her husband Yannis were the caretakers of the villa.

'Has the mail come yet?' Jennie asked Sofia, to break the horrible silence.

'No yet,' Sofia said. 'But I see Yannis coming up the hill. Will be soon.' And with a nod to each of them she rolled away to prepare their lunch. Jennie poured out two glasses from the jug which contained their own favourite mixture of gin, orange juice, and tonic water, and of course a great deal of ice, and handed one to Miles who accepted it with a grunt. Then she sat down in the chair next to him and sipped and stared at the impossibly blue sea, and watched out of the corner of her eyes for the level in his glass to sink to a point where she might reintroduce conversation.

At last, a third of the way from the bottom, he sighed and stretched his legs out before him and rubbed the back of his neck to relieve the tension. Jennie saw the lines of his face relax, and she smiled to herself, and Miles, catching the expression, asked her in a normal friendly voice, 'What's funny?'

'You are,' she said. 'I'm thinking of having you wired up—you know, like a doctor's consulting room, with those little lights that say "Enter" and "Wait"—only yours will say "Speak" and "Do not speak". It can be run automatically off your adrenalin gland.'

Miles grinned. 'Good morning, darling,' he said.

'Good morning, darling. Kiss.' They leaned across the gap between them and exchanged a kiss.

'What was it this time?' Jennie asked, replenishing their glasses. 'Not still chapter eight?'

'Yes,' Miles said, frowning. 'I've rewritten it three times already and it just won't come right.'

'What's the problem? Not Atkinson giving you trouble again?' Miles wrote immensely complicated spy stories featuring a Mycroft-Holmes-type figure called Atkinson who sat all day in a men's club and knew everything. His omniscience sometimes got in the way of the plot.

'No, I got rid of him at the end of chapter seven by sending his gall-bladder into hospital.'

'A device you can't use too often,' Jennie remarked, 'unless you want to kill him off.'

'Which might not be a bad idea, except that the public seems to like him.'

'For public read publisher. When did either of us ever find out what the public likes?'

'Speak for yourself,' Miles said loftily. 'My public writes to me.'

'Huh!' Jennie snorted. 'You mean that potty old clergyman in Norfolk writes to you, and then it's only to tell you that Mallory couldn't have reached London by eight o'clock because the train he caught doesn't connect with the London train at Peterborough and if he went via Chester he wouldn't have got in until eight twenty-three.'

'It isn't Norfolk, it's Lincoln.'

'It doesn't make him any less potty,' Jennie said. She drained her glass. 'Anyway, what is the problem?'

'I wondered when we'd get back to the subject,' Miles said. 'It's the usual trouble—getting the clues across. They've got to be there, and be accessible, but they mustn't be too obvious, so they've got to arise naturally out of the situations. Chapter eight's crucial, but I can't think of any natural way to introduce a dead lizard.'

Jennie wrinkled her nose. 'I'm not surprised. Can't you change it for something a little more mundane?'

'Not without rewriting the whole thing, and I'm behind schedule as it is.'

'I'm not,' Jennie said complacently. 'I did my three thousand words today. I should be finished by the end of the week.' Jennie wrote very popular historical romances. Miles glared at her.

'God, I hate you sometimes. You aren't in the least interested in my problem, are you?'

'Of course I am, darling,' Jennie smiled smugly. 'But it's your problem. I can't help you with it, other than by expressing concern.'

'That's another reason why I hate you,' Miles said gloomily. 'You're always right.'

'Never mind. Have some more lotion,' she said, reaching over with the jug. As she emptied the last of it into her glass, an old yellow retriever appeared at the end of the veranda and rolled slowly towards them, waving his tail and smiling a slobbery greeting. 'Ah, here's Wag. Yannis must be back with the mail,' Jennie said. 'Yes, yes, old thing, I love you too. Go and slobber on the master.' And she patted him and pushed him away. The old dog went to drop his muzzle on Miles's knee and stare up at him adoringly.

'Hello, old chap,' Miles said, rubbing the dog's ear affectionately. 'Did the nasty missus push you away then? She doesn't like you, Wag old man, that's what it is. She's a cruel hard woman, isn't she?'

'You and that dog,' Jennie observed dispassionately. 'He brings out the loony in you.'

'There's something basically wrong with a human being who doesn't like dogs,' Miles remarked equally casually.

'I couldn't love anything that smelled like that,' Jennie said. 'Besides, with Wag, love means wet.'

Miles grinned wickedly. 'So what's new?'

'Vulgar creature,' Jennie said, sticking her tongue out at him. He rubbed the now ecstatic Wag's ears again, while crooning to him.

'You see, old chap, the missus thinks love means never having to say you're soggy.'

'Yah!' Jennie said inelegantly, and then, as old Yannis appeared at the end of the veranda she called, 'Yasou, Yannis! Anything interesting today? What's the news from the village?'

Yannis placed the bundle of mail on the table between them, smiled a radiant smile full of broken teeth, and shuffled off backwards, calling the dog in Greek. He could rarely be persuaded to speak, though he knew English. His shyness was so chronic that Jennie wondered how he'd ever managed to marry and have children. At night from their quarters came only ever the sound of Sofia's voice speaking, and then a silence, then Sofia speaking again. Yannis was as silent with her as with everyone else.

Wag made half a turn to show willing to Yannis, but the veranda was cool and Miles was there, and lunch was coming soon, all factors of great weight with Wag, who was a great weight himself. With a final brace of tail-waves, he circled on the spot once and flopped down at Miles's feet. Miles was sorting the mail into two piles.

'Yours—yours—mine. What's this jiffy bag? Yours—feels like proofs.'

'Oh yes, that must be *On Eagle Crag*,' Jennie said. 'Damn, I hate reading my own books.'

'Who doesn't?' Miles said, still sorting. 'Yours—mine—mine—mine—yours—and the rest are mine.'

'Who doesn't what? Hate reading their own books, or hate reading my books?' Jennie asked suspiciously. Miles kept his eyes on his mail.

'What do you think?'

'That's what I thought. I know you, Egerton. You won't get away with this. I'll introduce a dead lizard to your bed in the most natural way you can imagine. That'll larn you.'

Miles blew her a kiss, and started opening his mail, and for a while there was no sound but the rustling of paper as they both read their letters. Moments later, Sofia arrived with another tray, bringing the first course of their lunch, and they had to shove aside their letters, opened and unopened, to make room on the table. Sofia had brought them an enormous bowl of Greek salad, a plate of golden-crusted chunky bread, and a bottle of very, very cold retsina. When she had departed again they continued to read while they ate and drank. It was Jennie's favourite time of the day. The delicious food after a morning's work, the first really good look at the sea, Miles's company, and the mail from England—what more could one want? Sometimes she missed home very badly, and she loved her letters, even when they were dull or bills. Miles looked upon his mail as a necessary nuisance. It was one of the many ways in which they differed.

He looked across now, and examined her mail upside down.

'What does Maurice want?' he asked, recognising the typeface. Maurice Heidsieck was Jennie's agent.

'Firmans have been on to him again. *The Eagle Flies* comes out in July and they're still keen to have me over there for a publicity tour. He says they've asked him to persuade me—as if Maurice could persuade me to do something I didn't want to!'

'Perhaps the bods at Firmans don't know you very well?'

'Not at all,' Jennie agreed. 'I've never met any of them in person. There wasn't any need. They took over the *Eagle* series from McKenzies when they bought them out and I just went on producing one every nine months.'

'Like breeding stock,' Miles said, smiling. 'Who is the top bod at Firman and Jackson anyway?'

'A bloke called Angus Mitchell. He was in charge of McKenzies' Scottish branch, in Glasgow, and when Firmans bought them and centralised the operation they put Mitchell in over the top of everyone.'

'I'll bet that lost him a few friends,' Miles remarked, poking around in the salad for the black olives. 'I wish Sofia could be persuaded to serve the olives separately. You did speak to her?'

'Twice. Ask her yourself—you might have more luck than me. It isn't that she refuses. She simply smiles and nods and then goes on doing things her own way after all.'

'Sounds like you, darling,' Miles said.

'Nonsense. I'm very biddable.'

'I'll bet poor old Maurice doesn't think so.'

'Maurice and I understand each other perfectly,' Jennie said with dignity.

'Oh, yes. He understands that what you say goes,' Miles said, taking some more bread. 'Who's the handwritten letter from?'

'I don't know—I haven't opened it yet.' Jennie dipped her bread in her wine and ate the soggy bit.

'Disgusting habits you have, Savage,' Miles said, wrinkling his aristocratic nose.

'Nothing disgusting about it—it's delicious. And it has a very respectable history. You've heard of sops?'

'What the dead used to give Cerberus?'

'The very same. Try some on Wag if you like.'

'No—he's soppy enough as it is.'

'Did you say soppy, or sloppy?'

'Yes.'

'That's what I thought,' Jennie said.

'Anyway, however ancient and noble they are, you don't have to eat like a medieval laird's wife, just because you spend your life writing about them.'

'Some of my life,' Jennie said, and Miles frowned at her. He never liked being reminded that she wrote three different series of novels under three different names, while he took a whole year and sometimes more to produce one of his spy thrillers. 'You shouldn't have married a writer, baby, if you don't like the competition,' she said now, watching his expression with faint amusement.

He looked round ostentatiously. 'I don't see the competition,' he said. 'Open your letter—I want to know who has that handwriting. It looks French or possibly even German.'

Jennie opened the letter, glanced at the end, and said, 'Of course, that explains it—it's from Bea Haviland.'

'Explains what?'

'The handwriting looking French. She was brought up in a convent.'

'Oh—Catholic?'

'Irish Catholic.'

'Do I know her?'

'I don't think you've actually met, but I've talked about her. She used to be assistant editor at Martin Mandersons when I used to write for them.'

'Oh yes, you have mentioned her. What's she doing now?'

'Well, she left Mandersons and went to work for Brain and Hamptons, but she didn't stay there very long. I think she left publishing actually, though I'm not sure what for.'

'And what does she want now?'

Jennie smiled at him in amused exasperation. 'How could I know? You haven't given me a chance to read her letter yet.'

'All right—get on with it then. More wine?'

He filled her glass while she read her letter. As with most things she did, she read very fast, and he watched her eyes flicking from side to side and down the page like a lizard's tongue. At the end she folded the letter and looked up at him speculatively.

'All right, what is it now?' he asked. 'You've got that look.'

'What look?'

'The one you wear when you're going to ask me something you think I won't like.'

'All right, Mister Mycroft Bleeding Holmes,' Jennie laughed. 'She wants to come and visit us. She's had an appendix operation, and she's recuperating, and she's been advised to get away from home and rest completely. She remembered that I now lived in Crete and thought we might be able to put her up.'

'How long for?' Miles asked.

'A month, she says. Here, read the letter for yourself.'

Miles waved it away. 'Can't be bothered. Girl-talk bores me.'

'Oh read it, you *poseur,* and let me catch up on my lunch.' She passed the letter across. 'And Wag, will you get your head off my feet? If I wanted my toes marinaded in saliva I'd do it myself.'

'Contortionist,' Miles said, taking the letter from her.

'Not as bad as Yannis. Yesterday he tied his ass to a tree and walked down to the village.'

Miles didn't laugh. That was the trouble with being married, Jennie thought, you knew each other's jokes too well. She watched Miles as he read the letter, as slowly and methodically as he wrote his books. *We're so different,* she thought. *I could never bear to take the pains he takes over his stuff. I suppose that's why I'll never be as good a writer as he is.* Having read the letter through, he turned the pages back and read it again. Jennie sighed. The pace of life in Crete suited Miles, though Jennie, even after five years, had never slowed down quite enough to match either her husband or the natives. There might be a word for *mañana* in Miles's vocabulary, but it wouldn't carry the same sense of urgency.

'Well?' he said, when he had finished his second reading.

'Well, what?'

'Well, are you going to ask her to stay?'

Jennie's eyebrows climbed her forehead. 'An odd question. I can't ask her just like that. It's for you to say.'

'Do you want her here?' he persevered.

'I'd like to see her again, but not so much that I'd want to impose her on you, if you don't want her.'

'A very circumspect answer, if I may say so, Watson. Well, if you want her, I don't mind. Might brighten us up a bit. But she'll have to understand about the working hours. I can't have her interrupting my work.'

'Nor mine,' Jennie said. She sometimes felt Miles didn't take her work seriously enough, dismissed it altogether too lightly. 'But I'm sure that won't be a problem. She can always lie around on the beach or go for drives. If she's recovering from an operation she may not even get up before midday.'

'Nevertheless, you'd better make sure she understands the set-up before she comes. I'm at a very crucial stage of my work.'

Jennie rolled her eyes. 'All right, Will.'

'Will?'

'Shakespeare.'

'Don't liken me to that hack,' he said severely. Jennie grinned.

'That's sacrilege. You can't call the world's greatest dramatist ever a hack.'

'Even if he was one?' Miles pleaded.

'Not even then, Egerton. You have no sense of the fitting. I suppose you think Jane Austen was just a woman novelist.'

'I know better than that,' he said scornfully. 'She was the woman who married that bloke, George Eliot, wasn't she?'

Jennie looked severe. 'One more word from you and I'll make you read the *Seven Pillows of Wisdom*.'

Miles shook his head. 'I didn't follow that one,' he said. It was a game they played, a game of instant associations.

'Perhaps it was a bit obscure,' Jennie apologised. 'I went from T.S. Eliot to T.E. Lawrence.'

'Oh, yes, now I'm with you. And from Lawrence to Laurence Durrell and thence to Gerald Durrell.'

'You got it, kid. Do I get a gold star?'

'You get two,' Miles said. 'Can I have the last olive?'

'Of course you can, my darling. Give me some more retsina. We'll have to ask Sofia for another bottle.'

'You'll get drunk.'

'Who ever got drunk on retsina?'

'You get drunk on wine.'

'Retsina doesn't count. Anyway, I had my fingers crossed.'

'Better cross your legs as well.'

'Now that really *is* obscure,' Jennie grinned, glad his humour was quite restored.

'What's she like, anyway?'

'She's fairly old, and fat, and she wears a black dress all the time, and a black—'

'Not Sofia,' Miles said patiently. 'This Bee woman.'

'The Bee-Woman. Sounds like science fiction. As I remember, she pronounces her name Bee-ah.'

'I don't like her. I don't like someone who can make two syllables out of Bea.'

'There are two in Beatrice,' Jennie pointed out. 'She's very pretty, and she used always to be very smart, dressed well—'

'You hadn't much in common then, I see.'

'Thanks. She's nice, anyway. I liked her.'

'But how close were you?'

'Not terribly. We had lunches, and I went to her home a couple of times. I liked her husband. They're split up now, of course.'

'Of course. Judging from our friends, it's become a national pastime.'

'Not us, though,' Jennie said happily, reaching under the table to squeeze his knee.

'Later, you wild, passionate thing.'

'Ooh Mr Pocock—Stanley, I mean. It's ever so exciting, being here alone with you at the Hotel Splendide.'

'Nothing mean about me, I hope,' Miles said, trying to insert his thumbs in a non-existent waistcoat. 'All right,' he said, reverting suddenly to his own persona, 'you can invite this woman. When's she coming?'

'A.S.A.P.,' Jennie said economically. 'You read the letter. It'll take my letter a few days to get to her, and then—'

'Send her a telegram.'

'You're keen to have her all of a sudden.'

'I want to get it over with.'

'Nuts. I know you.' Jennie eyed him closely. 'You're really pining for a bit of company, aren't you?'

'Well, if you want the honest truth—'

'A phrase which always ushers in a blatant untruth.'

'Just as "You can't miss it" means "You will certainly get lost".'

'No smoke screens. Just let me catch you making eyes at my friend, and I'll cut off your allowances.'

'You can't do that to me. You know you love me for my enormous potential.'

They smiled at each other, and Jennie said, 'There's nothing so nice as an old joke, is there?'

'There's nothing so old as an old joke,' Miles answered. 'It strikes me you might well ask the Bee-Woman to bring you out some new material when she comes.'

'You really mustn't start calling her the Bee-Woman, or it'll stick and you'll do it in front of her. It's Be-a.'

'All right, but be a little darling and call for Sofia. I want my next course.'

Jennie groaned at the pun, but got up anyway, and picked up the empty dishes to take with her and save a journey. As she passed Miles he reached out and touched the back of her hand, and she paused to look down at him and smile. The nice thing about marriage, she thought, was all the different ways you devised to communicate, as well as talking.

'Stop mooning,' Miles said, and swatted her firmly on the backside.

'Romance is dead,' she sighed, and removed herself from the target area.

CHAPTER TWO

REMEMBERING HOW Bea had always been smartly dressed, Jennie took a little trouble with her appearance on the day she went to meet her friend at the airport, and instead of the shapeless cotton dresses she normally wore for comfort's sake, she put on a pale green linen sundress with a matching short-sleeved jacket, and white sandals and a white straw hat.

'She's gone to your head,' Miles remarked as she passed him on the veranda. 'You're sure it's a woman you're meeting.'

'Would I go to this trouble for a man?' Jennie asked.

'Not even me,' Miles said gloomily.

'You can talk,' Jennie pointed out. Miles was wearing a pair of really revolting cut-offs and sandals with broken straps, and nothing else, and he hadn't shaved that morning. 'I hope you aren't going to greet poor Bea like that. She'll have a relapse.'

'I shan't greet her at all. I'll be asleep when she gets here. But I'll shave before I emerge, don't worry. That's why I didn't shave this morning, if you want to know.'

'You're an old darling really, aren't you?' Jennie said, leaning over to kiss him. 'Ugh. It's like kissing coconut matting.'

'You've never kissed coconut matting.'

'How do you know? You don't know what I used to get up to in my youth.'

'I've a fair idea. I've seen what you get up to in the youths of this island.'

'I should just about hope you haven't,' Jennie said laughing. 'I'll see you later, darling.'

It was about an hour's drive from Kritia to Iraklion where the island's only airport was situated, an hour's drive along the coast with some splendid views. Seeing it afresh now, imagining how it would strike Bea, Jennie fell in love with it all over again, as she had when Miles first brought her here on their honeymoon.

'I'm glad you like it,' he had said to her, 'because we're going to live here.' They had gone back to England after the honeymoon to settle things up, and then they had returned and lived in Crete ever since, first of all in a flat in Aghios Nicolaos while they were waiting for the villa to be built, and once it was finished, in the villa at Kritia, and neither of them had seen England since.

'I'll bet there've been some changes,' she thought, and wondered, with a sudden, painful pang, how it was that she had ever consented to leave her home country at all. Crete was beautiful, the Cretan people charming, but it wasn't home. It would be lovely to talk to someone from England, hear how things were now. She inched her foot down, and the battered old Triumph Herald convertible obediently found a burst of extra speed, and they skimmed along the new trunk road to Iraklion.

It was still early in the season and the airport was not yet crowded with tourists. The plane had not arrived yet, and Jennie stood back from the barriers with a little group of coach drivers and tour company couriers in their improbable uniforms and watched the surly airport staff lounging around, smoking and talking in loud, derisive voices. The people at the airport were the only Cretans she had met who were not charming, polite and friendly. Perhaps it was through spending their lives rubbing up against tourists. It was strange, she reflected, that though everyone went on holiday, and tourism was a major industry in almost every country, everyone still hated and despised holidaymakers.

A stir running through the group told her that the plane had touched down at last, and in a short while the visitors began to come through the gates, looking crumpled and sticky and disillusioned—all except one. The heads of the male airport staff jerked round after her like string puppets as she strode forward, looking fresh as a daisy and outrageously sexy. Her golden skin gleamed with health, her magnificent mane of hair, streaked with silver, hung down to her waist, her parma-violet boiler-suit was unbuttoned almost to the waist, revealing that she was certainly wearing no bra, and probably nothing else either, and she strode with a long-legged confidence which could have nothing to do with her puce sandals with four-inch heels that stayed on her feet by courtesy of one very thin strap across the toes.

Only belatedly, as the vision waved and called her name, did Jennie recognise Beatrice Haviland, and hastily change the gawp on her face for a welcoming smile. This was a woman recovering from an operation? Jennie, who had felt smart and pretty five minutes ago, felt about forty-five and haggard.

'Jennie darling! How lovely to see you again! You haven't changed a bit,' Bea cried, flinging her arms round a bemused Jennie and hugging her, and then standing back to survey her. She was wearing false eyelashes so thick and furry they looked like caterpillars, and her ears were pierced and she was wearing small gold studs in them.

'You've changed,' Jennie admitted. 'I didn't recognise you. You look marvellous. Where did you get that tan? I thought you'd been in hospital.'

'I have,' Bea said. 'This came out of a bottle. Man-Tan. It's gone streaky on my legs, that's why I'm wearing trousers. And the eyelashes are intended to hide the horrible marks under my eyes. Honestly, darling, when I looked at myself this morning, I was so horrified I nearly didn't come. I thought if I went out looking like that I'd make the flight crew sick, so I chucked on all this stuff. It helps a bit. I've got some sunnies in my bag, I'll chuck them on too when we get outside. I've got to keep my end up somehow when I meet your glorious husband.'

'How do you know he's glorious?' Jennie asked, amused.

'Oh, he must be! I've read all his books—I adore them. He *must* be glorious. Don't you absolutely adore his books?'

'I've never read them,' Jennie said. Bea stared.

'Why ever not?'

'It was a pact we made. We agreed I'd never read his books and he'd never read mine. Otherwise we'd probably find it impossible to restrain ourselves from offering criticism, and that's one thing a writer can't stand.'

'Really? That sounds terribly conceited.'

'Perhaps it does. But writers thrive on flattery, so if you tell Miles you adore his books, he'll probably purr and grow six inches taller and ask you to stay until Christmas.'

Bea grinned, showing lovely white teeth. 'Ah well, I don't think I'd mind that. If I never saw my office again, I wouldn't care a bit.'

'What is it you do now?' Jennie asked. 'I believe you left publishing.'

'I did. I work for the Irish Tourist Board now, at their information desk. Ah, sure, it's all right, and the money's good, but it isn't all that interesting. I'd sooner be back at Mandersons.'

'Why did you leave publishing then?'

'Money, darling, money. Why does anyone do anything in this benighted world? I have to have oodles of the stuff to keep my wardrobe full, and I have to have a full wardrobe to keep pulling the men.'

Jennie was amused. 'You have lots of men?'

'Got to, darling. Not only have I got an insatiable appetite, but men are all so dull nowadays, they don't last like they used to. In-built obsolescence like cars and furniture. Gone are the days, my old darling, when a man would last you twenty years or more, and still be in good enough condition at the end for a trade-in.'

'Stop! You're corrupting me,' Jennie said, laughing. 'I must say, though, that I like your new image. Your hair's different, isn't it? It used to be short and curly as I remember—'

'Oh, don't, I know what I looked like in those days. I weighed nine stone and wore pancake make-up. I had my hair straightened three years ago. Everyone seems to be perming these days, but my hairdresser told me if I had it permed after having it straightened it would shatter into tiny pieces and fall around my feet, so I had it streaked instead.'

'I like long hair, anyway,' Jennie said. 'What colour did it use to be?'

Bea looked blank. 'Damned if I remember. Oh look, there's my luggage coming through. Quick, it'll go round again.'

Taking all eyes with her, Bea ran (how?) across to the luggage conveyor and began wrestling with an outsize bright green suitcase. In seconds, four enormous muscular men appeared and gently moving her aside fought silently and politely with each other for her luggage while she smiled sweetly and directed them. In a moment she was walking demurely towards Jennie with the four men behind her, each carrying one of her bags.

'Have you got a car, Jen?' Bea asked, winking with the side of her face they couldn't see. 'I've got rather a lot of luggage.'

'Yes, out there,' Jennie said, and led the way, bemused. The men loaded Bea's bags into the back seat in grim silence, glaring at each other and simpering at her with a facial flexibility Jennie could only admire, and then when Bea had thanked them all effusively, they retired a pace or two to watch her get in and be driven away. Jennie, as far as they were concerned, was invisible.

'How glorious, an open car. I'd love to have one, but there's no point in London. I'm going to put my sunnies on. Do I need a scarf? Isn't it wonderfully hot here. I'll be tanned in no time.'

Chattering happily, she rummaged in her enormous leather

handbag and produced a pair of sunglasses which, once in place, obscured most of her face, and then she leaned back and enjoyed the drive. Jennie, watching the wind whip back that mane of silver-streaked hair, thought she looked like the model for an advertisement. I have let time pass me by, she mused.

'I'd better explain the routine at the villa to you, Bea,' Jennie said after a pause, 'because Miles mustn't be disturbed at his work or he's impossible to live with.'

'Oh, I can understand that. I'm sure it must be very difficult being a genius. I wouldn't disturb his work for the world. I'm only terribly grateful to you for having me here at all. It's really wonderful of you both.'

'I shall enjoy the company,' Jennie said. 'But the thing is, everyone in Crete siestas from about two in the afternoon until about five, and so everything has to be planned around that. Miles and I get up early, and we work from eight until one. Then we lunch, we siesta until around five, shower, have a cup of tea and so on. Sometimes we do a bit more work in the evening, if we're behind. Dinner is around eight, and that tends to go on a bit. The Cretans can make dinner last from eight until three in the morning without any apparent strain.'

'It sounds marvellous,' Bea said. 'What do you do for entertainment?'

Jennie smiled a little. 'In Crete?'

'Oh! Like that, is it?'

'The only form of outside entertainment really is eating. Our nearest town is Aghios Nikolaos—Ag Nick, we generally call it. There's a disco there, I believe, and some of the restaurants have dancing and music at night. Sometimes we have friends to dinner, and sometimes we go out for a meal. Otherwise I'm afraid you'll find it a bit quiet. But after all, that's what you came for, isn't it—a rest?'

'Don't worry, Jen, I shall love it, I'm sure. Just lounging around on the beach and so on. Who needs entertainment?'

'That's what Miles always says. I agree up to a point, but there are times when I pine for a good play, or a concert, or one of those witty dinner parties I used to love in London, with beautifully dressed people saying impressively clever things between courses.'

Bea laughed at that. 'I don't think I ever went to one,' she said. 'All the parties I went to ended up with someone being sick, or two someones having a blazing row about politics, or four someones getting off with each others' partners. I shall be glad to get away from them, at any rate. But tell me, who do you have to your parties?'

'Exiles like ourselves. There aren't too many, but there are a few on the island who are invitable. There's Andrew who runs a tourist shop down in the village—he's a painter, and very nice. You'd like him. And then the couple who run the big hotel on the bay—the Smithsons. And another writer who lives out at Zakros, and his wife.' They sounded horribly dull to Jennie even as she mentioned them. A passionate longing swept through her for the free, exciting life she imagined Bea lived in London. But then Bea pricked the bubble by saying, 'You are so *lucky,* Jen, living here on this beautiful island, with a husband who loves you, and just a few friends. London's such a pit, and the people are just ravening beasts, all mouth and claws, and so boring after the first dozen. All want, want, want. I could do with some peace and quiet. And perhaps a bit of sincerity.'

'We'll see what we can do,' Jennie said, reaching out and patting her hand. 'Poor Bea. We must cure you of your disillusionment. But, look! There's the villa,' Jennie exclaimed, pulling off the road on to the cliff edge where the road skirted a headland. Below them was the bay, and the village of Kritia, little more than a few peasant houses and two hotels, but boasting a sandy beach which is a rarity in Crete. The land rose steeply from it to the road and was terraced and planted with vines, still tiny, tender-leaved stumps in the rich red earth. Above the road, the land sloped more shallowly, and there were olives as far as the eye could see, interspersed with almond trees in full blossom and here and there tall dark cypresses, male and female. Farther up still, the land grew steep again, and little grew but gorse, its bloom like yellow sparks against its dark foliage, and then at last was the scarp of the mountain-top rising to the cloudless sky.

The pattern was repeated again and again on almost every headland, and on the headland opposite them now, at the top of the cliff where the road ran, was the pale blue villa, nestling in its frame of trees, dark-leaved orange and lemon trees, and fat silvery carobs, and brooding cypress.

'Oh, it's so pretty!' Bea exclaimed, and Jennie nodded, drawing a breath of pleasure even after so long.

'It is, isn't it? I still stop here every time to look at it. It's the only place from which you can see it. I love the way it's tucked in there, like a patch of fallen sky.'

'I've never seen a house painted that colour before,' Bea said.

'It's said to be the colour the gods love,' Jennie said. 'The olive grove above the house belongs to us, and the vines on the terraces below. And we have goats, of course, and chickens, and two donkeys, an old one called Jude, and a young one called Philomena.'

Bea was almost clasping her hands in rapture. 'It's just heavenly. I don't think I shall ever want to go away again.'

Jennie looked at her curiously. 'Do you know, those were almost my exact words when Miles first brought me here.'

'How on earth do you manage to look after all those animals and the farmland as well as everything else you have to do?'

'I don't,' Jennie said, amused. 'We have a couple. He tends the trees and she tends the beasts.'

Bea looked shocked. 'Servants? You have servants? Jennie, how can you square that with your conscience?'

'I don't know. I don't seem to have any trouble about it. Anyway, I don't think Sofia and Yannis regard themselves as servants.'

'All the same—'

'All the same what? You can't really think Miles would be able to rush out at dawn to plant things before coming back to write his books—'

'Oh no, of course not. I didn't expect him to do it.'

'You expected me to do it? It's all right for me to do those things, but not for Sofia and Yannis?'

'But you wouldn't be paid,' Bea explained.

'I can't see how that makes it better,' Jennie said, baffled. 'Well, anyway, I want something to drink. Let's get home.' She would sooner end this conversation now before it got into any deeper water, and she put the old Herald into gear and shot off round the last few bends to the villa.

Miles was still asleep when they arrived, though it was just after five, and so Jennie showed Bea quietly to her room, speaking in a whisper out of old habit. Bea was satisfyingly pleased with everything. She loved her room, which was cool and dim behind closed shutters. The walls were distempered a pale apple green and the bedspread and rugs were slightly darker shades of green to blend in. The floor, like the floors throughout the house, was plain parquet, and the adjoining bathroom was also in green, with great pots of ferns everywhere.

'It's lovely, absolutely perfectly lovely,' Bea whispered fervently. 'And a private bathroom too—how posh!'

'There's one to every bedroom. It's a necessity really, with the heat in the summer. It isn't bad now, but in July and August you have to shower about every five minutes.'

Bea had taken off her dark glasses, and now, in the dimmer light, Jennie could see how tired and worn she looked, with dark patches under her eyes and a sunken look to her cheeks.

'Look, Bea,' Jennie said, 'why don't you take your things off, have a nice cool bath, or a shower, and then lie down on the bed for a couple of hours. You'll feel much more like enjoying the evening when you've had a little sleep.'

'But I never sleep during the day,' Bea said unconvincingly.

'You'll be surprised how quickly you pick up the habit, living here. You look very tired. I'll bet if you just lie down and relax for a few minutes you'll drop off.' Reading Bea's mind, she added, 'You won't be missing anything. We'll just sit around doing nothing, or write letters for a couple of hours. I'll call you in time to get ready for dinner, how about that?'

'All right,' Bea said, giving in without too much struggle. She really was tired. 'But I'd love something to drink first, if you don't mind. I'm so thirsty.'

'All right. You get under the shower, and I'll bring you in some orange juice.'

Jennie took her time getting the orange juice, to give Bea a chance to have her shower, and only when she heard the water being turned off did she make her way to Bea's bedroom. She went in quietly. Bea was lying on the bed, her damp towel round her, and though her eyelids flickered when Jennie approached her, they soon dropped again. Smiling, Jennie put the glass down on the bedside table, and drew the damp towel out from under Bea's body and hung it over the back of a chair. Bea murmured, turned on her side, and was asleep before Jennie was out of the room.

'Well, what's she like?' Miles asked when Jennie went into their bedroom. It was much like the green room, except a little bigger, and the predominant colour was a soft lilacy blue. Miles was sitting up on the bed, leaning against the wall with his hands behind his head. He had just woken, and looked rumpled and sticky-eyed.

'Different from the way I remembered her,' Jennie said after a moment's thought.

'Different better or different worse?'

'Just different. She's very pretty, and her clothes seem very fashionable.'

'Only seem?' Miles asked.

'Well, I don't know what fashions are like in England any more, but if they aren't fashionable, I can't account for them.'

'Do I detect a note of envy in your voice, Savage?' Miles asked, grinning at her.

'She made me feel forty and frumpish,' Jennie said. 'But I

shall fight back. She's the same age as me, I know for a fact, and if she can do it, I can. At least my tan's genuine.'

'Dear me, she seems to be bringing out a very unhealthy streak of competition in you.'

'Don't be so smug. What's unhealthy about competition anyway?'

'It depends what you're competing about. Are you afraid you'll lose me to her?'

'You make it sound as if I'm going to gamble with her using you as a stake. *Lose* you indeed! Such language, and from a man to whom language ought to be a tool.'

'Osmosis,' he explained. 'Living side by side with your ghastly *ro*mances.' He emphasised the first syllable, which made it sound worse. 'Eventually it's bound to have an effect.'

'All right,' Jennie said. 'I shall have my revenge. Don't forget you're five years older than me, and if she makes me feel like forty she's going to have a terrible effect on your gonads. Your clothes are even worse than mine, and your hair needs cutting.'

Miles got up from the bed and looked lofty. 'I shall ignore those aspersions on my character. What interest could I have in a chit of a girl, however she's dressed? I shall make no concessions to her. I shall shave and shower, as I would have anyway, and I shall put on the clothes I would have worn to dine with you. She won't alter my life, I can tell you.'

'Garn,' Jennie said derisively.

'You don't believe me?' he said, pretending to be hurt.

'You haven't seen her.'

'That won't make any difference.'

'I'll believe you,' Jennie said. 'But the first time I see you preen yourself—' She let the sentence trail away, and walked round the bed to put herself in his arms. When they woke from siesta was the time they had sex, when they had sex, although it wasn't every day any more as it was when they were first married. Quite apart from the fact that the excitement wore off after a while, they were both working so hard that it took up a great deal of the energy they would otherwise have put into more frivolous things. But, whether it was a reaction to the challenge of Bea or not, Jennie wanted him now. She pressed herself against his familiar body, tilting her face to be kissed.

He kissed her, but she knew instantly it was no good. His hands on her shoulders were impersonal, his mouth kissing hers was performing a ceremony. She sighed, and drew back. In the early days of their marriage she had sometimes persevered when he wasn't in the mood, but even then it had never done any good. When he didn't want to, he didn't want to, and there was absolutely nothing one could do about it. After five years of marriage she no longer flogged dead horses, and when she met with this blank reaction to her wanting him she simply turned over and went to sleep. It was disappointing, and in the beginning it had been hurtful before she had told herself that it wasn't an intentional slight and that one couldn't help not being in the mood sometimes, that after all sex wasn't everything—there was more to marriage than that.

'Are you going to have your shower now?' she asked as she turned away.

'Yes, and my shave—don't worry, I won't let you down.'

'I'll have a bath then, and keep you company. Bea's asleep—she looked wrecked when she arrived, so I suggested she have a shower and then lie down for a while, and she was off as soon as her head touched the pillow. I'll wake her for dinner, so we'll have a little time to ourselves.'

'Oh,' Miles said, and he sounded for a moment almost disappointed. Then, 'Good idea, really. Travelling's very tiring. You're going to be tired too, missing your siesta.'

'I'll live,' Jennie smiled. She got into the bath while Miles showered, and watched him as he busily soaped himself and then shaved. She liked to see him with no clothes on. He had a good body, lean and almost boyish, with sweet fair skin, dusted with freckles over his shoulders. He had never been very muscular, no he-man, but he had never, on the other hand, got fat or sloppy. His hair was thinning now, but doing it politely from the front backwards; he wouldn't have a bald patch on the top of his head like a monk, a thing she didn't care for. His face was firm, and a tan suited him, and the remoteness of his eyes was as attractive now as it had always been.

She still wanted him. She timed her bath to his movements, and was out and drying herself at the same moment as him. Perhaps proximity would do the trick. He turned at last from the mirror and looked into her face, and then smiled and came forward and put his hands on her shoulders. They might have been the hands of a different man from the last time. She quivered.

'I think you ought to go to bed for a while, Mrs Egerton,' he said softly. 'You'll be tired later.'

'I hate going to bed alone,' she sighed. 'If only I had some company.'

He stepped closer and kissed her, and this time he closed his eyes and did it properly. Her towel fell from her body, and she felt his naked flesh harden against her. In a moment he stopped kissing her, took her hand, and led her to the bed, and she stretched herself out and held up her arms to him, and received his familiar warmth and weight happily against her. Every movement was familiar, known from a hundred previous occasions, every movement, every gesture, every word, every sound. We could do this in our sleep, she caught herself thinking, and was shocked at herself.

'Darling,' she murmured into his ear to compensate for her wandering mind.

'I love you, Jennie,' he whispered back, and at the words her stomach knotted, and there was no more need to worry about her thoughts. His loving her was the most exciting thing about him, and she clung to him with real passion as they worked out the well-known pattern.

CHAPTER THREE

WHEN BEA had been at the villa a fortnight, Jennie decided to give a party, just to break the monotony for her. She was a little worried that Bea might be finding it dull, although she gave no sign of boredom.

'But she might be hiding it out of politeness,' she said to Miles at breakfast one morning. Bea was not there—she never appeared at breakfast, and Jennie was rather glad, for she liked the quietness of the early morning and having Miles to herself. The sea was a remote, misty lavender, the sky as tender a blue as flax flowers, and the cool, dewy sunshine sloped between bars of long shadow from the surrounding trees. The air was scented delicately with flowers and resin, smells that were burnt out later in the day by the heat, and the quietness seemed to have a shining quality in which the distant fall of the waves and the sounds of birds and insects were minutely, crystally clear.

Miles poured them each another cup of fragrant coffee and then reached out for a crisp roll which he spread lavishly with butter and Cretan heather-honey.

'I shouldn't worry about her,' he said. 'She can tell you if she's bored. And if she doesn't show any signs of it, there's no point in inventing troubles for yourself.'

'Does that mean you don't want a party?' Jennie enquired, peeling an orange. Miles gave a quirky smile.

'You women!' he said to annoy her. 'You never ask what you want to ask. And you never accept an answer as saying what it says.'

'That's because *you men* never say what you really mean,' Jennie replied in mind.

'Have a party, by all means. It's probably about time we had another. We ought to fulfil our share of social responsibility.'

'We do,' Jennie said. 'As I remember, we gave the last one. But who's counting? Okay, I'll ask people today.'

'You don't sound overjoyed at the prospect.'

'It's only the thought of spending the morning wrestling with the Cretan telephone system.'

'Don't wrestle then. It's probably just as quick to walk down to the village and ask people in person.'

'And leave my work for the morning?' Jennie said, pretending to be scandalised.

'You're always banging on about how far ahead you are. You shouldn't mind a day off. What are you doing at the moment, anyway?'

'Well I still haven't read those proofs. I keep putting them off.'

'Put them off again,' Miles said. 'Who cares?'

'Firman and Jackson, presumably,' Jennie said. 'You seem keen to get me out of the way, Egerton. I'm on to you—you want to be left alone with Bea for the morning.'

Miles beat his forehead. 'Curses! Found out again! You're too clever for me, my darling. I can't get away with anything.'

'Well, if that's all it is, I'll definitely go down to the village. If I tell Andrew who we're going to invite, he can telephone from his shop those people who don't live on the bay.'

Miles laughed. 'Dear old Andrew! Always get him to do your dirty work.'

'He hasn't much else to do. And for some reason his telephone always works better than ours. Maybe it's because he's in the village on a main line, or something.'

'Maybe it's because the operator's in love with him.'

'Is she?'

'How should I know? But all the middle-aged lonely women in Crete seem to home in on his shop for half an hour's sympathy.'

'Andrew's a very nice person,' Jennie said defensively. Miles merely smiled. 'Don't be so superior. You could do with a bit of his niceness.'

'He could do with some of my talent, but he's never likely to have it.'

A retort came to Jennie's lips but she bit it back. There was no future in quarrelling over Andrew, of whom Miles had always been, for reasons best known to himself, contemptuous. At first Jennie had thought Miles might be jealous, although there had never been anything other than a long-standing and very platonic friendship between her and Andrew. Later she had simply stopped wondering. They were just different people, she supposed.

'I think I'll go and see if Bea's awake, and tell her. Give her something to think about,' Jennie said, and left Miles to his week-old *Sunday Times*.

In the cool gloom of the green bedroom, Jennie saw that Bea was awake, lying on her back under a single sheet and staring at the ceiling with a half smile on her face.

'Hullo,' Jennie said. 'I'm not disturbing you?'

'No,' Bea said. 'I was just daydreaming.'

'It looked like a good one. What's his name?' Jennie said.

'I wouldn't like to tell you,' Bea said. 'Did you want something?'

'Only to tell you I've decided we'll give a party tomorrow night. I thought you might be finding things a bit dull.'

'Oh, no,' Bea said emphatically. 'I'm having a lovely time. But a party would be lovely too.'

'Good. I'm going down into the village this morning to

issue the invitations and organise things. Would you like to come with me?'

Bea removed her gaze from the ceiling and looked at Jennie rather oddly, she thought. She opened her mouth to speak, shut it again, and then said casually, 'No thanks. I don't think I could stand that long trek in the heat.'

'We could take the donkeys,' Jennie said. She rather fancied some company. 'And then I could introduce you to Andrew. He's awfully nice.' It would be a good thing, she thought, if she could get Bea off with Andrew—good for both of them. Andrew was far too nice a person to remain single and lonely.

'I'll meet him at the party, won't I? Don't let's spoil the surprise. Anyway, if there's to be a party I must spend the day on my suntan.'

Jennie resigned herself. 'You're looking better, I must say, for the rest.'

'I feel better. Jen—' Bea pushed herself up on to her elbows and became suddenly earnest. 'I really am grateful for the good care you're taking of me. I wish—'

'Mm?'

'Oh, nothing. I really do love being here, Jen. I wish I could stay for ever. You go off and plan the party. I think it's a super idea. I shall spend the whole day planning what to wear, and stun all your friends.'

'You'll do that anyway,' Jennie said, smiling. 'Our circle haven't seen anything like you since John Smithson had a private showing of *Dr No* with Ursula Andress in his hotel. Be careful of the sun if you're sunbathing. Don't overdo.'

Bea smiled. 'You say that every day. I won't, don't worry.'

Jennie left her, wondering if she was becoming a bore. Everyone kept telling her she was always repeating herself. She felt restless suddenly, and longed for a change of scene and a change of company. That was the trouble with living abroad, the circle from which you could draw your friends was so limited that it was hard to find anyone you could really get fond of. Andrew was an exception, of course, but then she had known Andrew before they came to Crete.

It had been one of the reasons that they had settled on Kritia for their villa. Andrew Lennon was a painter, and Jennie had met him when he was teaching at the Chelsea College of Art and she was at university. They had accepted bedsitters in the same house, and after weeks of passing each other on the stairs and competing politely for the same bathroom they had struck up a friendship which had been Jennie's mainstay at a time when she had few friends and felt at a loss in the big city. Andrew had fed her when her grant ran out, and she had reciprocated by playing chess with him and talking all through the long nights when he couldn't sleep and was desperate for company.

They had lost touch when Jennie had finished college, and she learnt later that he had gone abroad to further his career as a painter. When she and Miles had honeymooned in Crete, they had discovered Andrew running his little tourist shop where he sold his own paintings along with various up-market craft items, and she had gladly renewed their former friendship. He seemed to have given up hope of ever being a great painter, but he seemed reasonably content, except for a deep-seated vein of sadness which he hardly ever allowed to show, but which Jennie sensed and was sorry for, though she did not know its cause.

Jennie dressed in shorts and a T-shirt for her trip to the village because she had decided to ride Philomena, since it would be hot when she returned and the hill was steep. Philomena, the little chocolate-coloured female donkey, was unwilling to part from Jude and the goats, and made as much noise as if she were being slowly strangled, causing Miles to appear with an expression of extreme irritation to demand, unreasonably, if this sort of thing was going to go on all day, and Sofia to appear more constructively to smack Philomena on the behind with her wooden spoon and berate her in Greek. Philomena recognised the hand that fed her and became instantly tractable, fluttering her eyelashes seductively and looking as though butter wouldn't melt. Jennie smiled her thanks, vaulted astride the little ass's shoulders, and set off down the dusty white track.

The road was shaded for much of the way by the great, fat-trunked carob trees that grew on either side, and by the orange trees, still bearing the last of their glowing golden harvest. Spring in Crete was wonderful for the greenness of everything—which late in the year would be burnt to brown by the fierce sun—and the wonderful variety of the wild flowers that crammed themselves into every possible cranny which contained even a speck of earth. The colours were wonderful—scarlet poppies, purple mallow, crimson bugloss, three different colours of vetch trailing like pea-plants along the grass edge. Furry cats-ears and giant daisies grew at the bottoms of walls where dampness collected; in drier places there were geraniums of every colour from apple-blossom pink to deepest vermilion.

The dry-stone wall that held the uphill terrace along the side of the road sported wigs of rock-cress and sea-pinks, and above them the giant cacti were in bloom with flowers of improbable colours the size of dinner plates. Higher up the hillsides there were pale-blue painted hives, and the bees worked industriously amongst wide-spreading clumps of flowering thyme and sage.

As they came down into the village there were more houses, stone for the most part and painted white, but with so many rickety additions of wood and corrugated iron that it was often hard to see the original structure. The Cretan people loved flowers, and any old tin or box or other receptacle that would hold a little earth was put to the use of a flower-pot to grow geraniums and vines and carnations and daisies. People waved to her as she rode past, and called cheerful greetings, for she was well known after five years' residence. Now she was in the village itself, pattering through the narrow streets with their secret, dark houses and tiny dusty shops. Philomena stepped neatly round a yellow cur-dog that was basking in a strip of sunshine in the middle of the road, and as they passed the fishmonger's shop Jennie saw a ginger cat sitting patiently in the doorway watching the fishmonger gut giant dogfish.

Andrew's shop was on the harbour front, with the other

tourist shops selling Greek vases, cotton blouses, copper utensils, and Cretan rugs, and the more expensive restaurants. There were few tourists about this early in the morning, but nonetheless all the shops were open. Jennie hitched Philomena in the shade of a carob and strolled across to the door of Creta Studios.

'Anyone home?' she called. 'I've come to buy a Picasso.'

Andrew came through from the back and smiled a very pleased greeting.

'Hullo! Was it his blue period you were after?'

'It wouldn't go with my rinse. Have you got the same thing in pink?' It was one of their old routines. Andrew came forward to kiss her, chastely, but on the lips. Over the years his greeting had moved from her cheek to her mouth, and was lasting a fraction longer every year.

'Now I know it's you,' he said. 'How are you? How is everything? It's weeks since I saw you. Is everything all right?'

'Of course,' she said. 'How should it not be?'

'You looked anxious when you came in.'

'I'm not. I'm fine. Is there any coffee?'

'Of course there's coffee. Come through. It's lovely to see you again.'

He took her hand to lead her through to the back room, though it was not necessary. Jennie thought he just liked the contact. The sun was on that side of the building, and the back room was sunlit and pleasant. The room was a combination of kitchen and sitting room, sporting a wooden table and chairs and a sofa and easel towards which Jennie went immediately while Andrew went to the stove for the coffee.

'What is it this time?' Jennie asked, walking round the easel to look at the part-finished painting. She always hoped it would be something important, that Andrew would have begun working again. She was disappointed this time as always before.

'Oh, just more tourist rubbish,' Andrew called over his shoulder. It was a typically Cretan foreshore, done in Andrew's bold but careful style and meticulously accurate colouring. Jennie thought it was very good, but she had learnt over the years not to praise Andrew's paintings, for he hated her to like the things he did for tourists, which he regarded as his failure to be a 'real' painter.

'Pity,' she said now. 'I thought you might be working again.'

He made a face at her as he came back with the coffee. 'You didn't,' he said. 'You hoped I might be, but you didn't think I was. I'll never paint again, Jennie, you ought to know that. I haven't got it in me.'

'Oh, balls,' she said crossly. 'You shouldn't be so defeatist. Look at me—a hack, but I still think one day I'll write a great book. And I'm a damned good hack, and proud of it. You do better hack paintings than anyone else in the world, so why be ashamed? The time isn't right yet, that's all.'

Andrew touched the back of his hand to her cheek. 'You'd never have made RADA,' he said. 'But thanks all the same.'

'Which means change the subject,' Jennie said, holding his eyes for a moment. Andrew was really astonishingly good looking, fair, bronzed and brown-eyed, and yet one never noticed it. He managed always to give the impression of being plain and rather dull as far as looks went, just as, mysteriously, Miles, who hadn't a good feature in his face, always managed to give the impression of being marvellously handsome. She must have been staring too much, for Andrew suddenly withdrew his gaze with a suspicion of embarrassment, and turning away from her to sugar his coffee he said:

'To what do I owe the honour of this visit, anyway? The grapevine tells me that you have a visitor up at the villa.'

'Good old grapevine. Yes, it's an old friend of mine, Bea Haviland. She's recuperating from an appendix operation, and I thought I'd give a party tomorrow night to cheer her up.'

'Does she need cheering up?'

'Well, not exactly,' Jennie admitted. 'In fact she seems to have made herself extremely at home. She gets up for lunch, spends the afternoon sunbathing, chatters brightly and sophisticatedly through dinner, and then reads to us out of *Winnie the Pooh* on the veranda under the stars.'

Andrew cocked his head shrewedly. 'Discontent bristles all over you. Why is she putting your nose out of joint?'

'She isn't. I'm very fond of her,' Jennie said. Andrew waited. 'All right,' she said at last, 'but it isn't anything to do with her. I just feel restless all of a sudden.'

'Is she pursuing Miles?' he said abruptly, as if he had just thought of it. Jennie smiled at the idea.

'Oh, no, of course not. She hero-worshipped him for the first two days, because she'd read all his books, but once she discovered he was an ordinary human being with dirty toenails and hair that needs cutting she relaxed with him. They get on like old friends now.'

Andrew raised an eyebrow. 'Young? Pretty?'

'The same age as me. And ravishingly pretty.'

'Hm. I think a party would be a good idea. Bring her into range of some other men. Am I to come?'

'Darling Andrew, of course you are. You are always the first person I invite.'

He smiled ruefully, but he said only, 'And who else?'

'Well I wondered if you'd do a bit of telephoning for me. You know how my phone is; yours is much more reliable. I'll call in on the Smithsons while I'm here, and anyone else who lives in the village, but I thought you could ask the others for me.'

'Just give me a list,' he said. That was the nice thing about Andrew, he never made a fuss about doing things for you.

'Well, Ben Hyssop and Caroline, of course, and James Laurence and Lisa,' Jennie said, naming the other writers on the island, 'and Alex, and Jane Scott, and the Wellses—'

'All the old crowd, in fact, Andrew said. 'All right, Jennie, I'll do that for you today. Are you going to have some entertainment?'

'Oh, yes, I thought Bea would like to see some Cretan dancing, and listen to the local music. I'll fix that up, though, don't you worry. Oh, and I wonder, if I order the booze, could you collect and bring it up with you tomorrow? You'll come early, won't you?'

'As early as you like,' he said gravely.

'And wear something really nice, something sexy,' Jennie said. 'You're so good looking, and you've got a lovely figure. You never make the most of it, and I want to impress Bea with how handsome my friends are.'

Andrew smiled at that. 'It's no use trying to get me off with your new little friend, Jennie, it won't work.'

'How do you know?' Jennie said reasonably. 'You haven't met her yet. Give it a chance. She'd liven you up. She'd be very good for you.'

'Stop matchmaking, it isn't attractive. I don't want to be livened up, and I doubt that she'd be good for me. She'd disturb me, and demand all sorts of attentions I wouldn't want to give her.'

'You are *difficult* sometimes, Andrew,' Jennie sighed. 'I wonder if you've been having a secret love affair all these years—you seem so impervious to other women.'

Andrew merely smiled at that.

'Well, I'd better get on and ask the others. I'll see you tomorrow then, if I don't see you before?'

Having called in on John and Kay Smithson at the hotel, where she managed to offload another batch of invitations which they agreed to pass on for her, Jennie went to the inner harbour to seek out an old fisherman by the name of Nikos, who was the leader of a troupe of musicians and dancers who provided most of the live entertainment in those parts. There was, surprisingly, not much, and most places relied on taped Greek music featuring endless repetitions of 'Zorba's Dance' and 'Never on a Sunday', two tunes it was assumed no tourist could do without on a visit to any part of Greece.

Jennie found Nikos mending a net in the sun on the harbour-side. His boat was tied up before him. He still sailed one of the old fashioned wooden fishing boats with the enormous beaked prow and the two blue eyes painted one on either side of it. The blue eyes were the Eyes of God, which were meant to protect fishermen from evil. Nikos was a villainous old man with a dirty beard, long fingernails, and the glittering eyes of a pirate. He spoke little English, but nevertheless seemed to understand it well enough—perhaps too well. He was thoroughly unreliable, but he could play any instrument man had invented, and bring magic out of it, and without him the troupe would not have functioned at all.

Jennie greeted him in Greek out of courtesy, gave him the gift of tobacco she had brought, and then sat down on the harbour wall near him and waited. It was never any good trying to hurry a Cretan, and with Nikos you simply had to wait until he wanted to speak to you. Try to speak to him first, and he would simply become blind and deaf. He took the tobacco without comment, examined it minutely, turning the package over and over in his hands, rubbing it with his fingers and hefting it to test it for weight. Then he raised it to his face and snuffed it all over like a dog, and then he pushed it inside his jersey, spat politely away from Jennie, and resumed his work. Another five minutes, and he looked up at her with his bright slitty eyes and made an interrogative noise.

Relieved, Jennie made her request, that the whole troupe should be engaged to come up to the house and play music for the evening, and to give a display of dancing towards the end of the evening when the guests were lit up enough to let themselves go and enjoy it. The negotiations were slow, and once he had agreed to do it there was a long-drawn-out discussion over the money, at the end of which the price was fixed at the figure he always received. This sort of thing maddened Jennie almost beyond endurance. She liked quick, direct decisions, and the long haggling when both of them knew the eventual outcome seemed utterly pointless. Yet she had had to learn to be patient, for had she offered him that sum straight off he would have been so offended he would have refused the engagement and probably would never have performed for her again.

Everything settled, Jennie made herself sit with him in silence for another five minutes before saying goodbye and walking away with such relief she had to stop herself from running. She made a few more calls, including one to the off-licence to order the drinks for Andrew to bring with him the next day, and then, worn out, she retraced her steps to the patient Philomena and set off home. Philomena pattered along gladly, always happier to go home than to leave it, and Jennie was able to daydream along, having no need to give the donkey any directions.

It was almost lunch time when she arrived back at the villa, and everything was very quiet—unnaturally quiet, she thought, for as she turned Philomena loose and walked round to the back of the villa, she could not hear the usual clattering of Miles's typewriter. She went to his room and found it empty, and, puzzled, she sought out Sofia in the kitchen.

'Mr Miles gone swimming,' Sofia told her expressionlessly, 'with the young lady.'

'Really?' Jennie said, surprised. Miles never liked to disturb his work schedule and she hoped fervently that Bea hadn't gone and bothered him and badgered him into accompanying her. 'Did they go down to our own beach?'

Sofia shrugged. 'They say they come back for lunch. I don't know.'

'Well, never mind,' Jennie said. 'I wanted to talk to you about the party tomorrow. We shall need some nice things to eat.'

Sofia brightened at that. She loved parties, and she loved cooking, and Jennie knew that she would put everything she had into the preparations. 'And your two sons will dance with the troupe, I hope,' Jennie added. Sofia glowed. Her two youngest sons were her pride and joy.

'Yes, yes, they will dance. I polish up their chains tonight and I tell them clean their boots. They will make you proud, kyria.'

'Of course they will,' Jennie said warmly.

She was on the terrace drinking her second long cocktail when the voices of Miles and Bea wafted up the steep steps from the beach. They arrived on the terrace with their damp towels over their shoulders and broad smiles on their faces, and Jennie merely raised an eyebrow at Miles, who smirked self-consciously.

'We've had an absolutely luscious swim, Jen,' Bea greeted her exuberantly. 'We swam to that cave, and Miles showed me the crystals. What colours! I wish I could have a bit mounted.'

'Get everything done, darling?' Miles said. 'Everything fixed up?'

'Yes, thanks,' Jennie said. 'But what about you? I hope your work won't get behind?'

Miles looked more sheepish than ever, but passed it off airily. 'Oh, I thought as long as you were having a day off, I would too. I was getting stale, ploughing away at the same chapter day after day.'

'Oh, I see,' Jennie said, and left it at that. Bea looked from one to the other with an odd, quirky smile.

'Poor old Jen's pissed off because we've been enjoying ourselves while she's been working. Never mind, Jennie darling, if you like I'll do everything tomorrow, and you can lounge about and give me orders like a housemaid. How will that be?'

'Don't be silly,' Jennie smiled. 'There won't be all that much to do, anyway. Sofia will see to the food, and Andrew's bringing the drink, and I've arranged the entertainment. You are to be treated to a display of Cretan dancing, such as you will never see anywhere else but *chez* Egerton. And I want you to be a good girl and take care of Andrew for me tomorrow, because if he's not watched he puts himself into a corner and does maddeningly helpful things like serving food and washing glasses, and then goes home early. I want him to enjoy himself.'

It was clumsily done, Jennie realised, as soon as she said it, and it deserved the reception it got. Miles put her down instantly by saying, 'I've never known old Andrew go home before dawn when there's a party going. Last time we had to go to bed before he'd take the hint.'

And Bea said, 'It's no use, Jennie old thing, Miles has been telling me about this secret lover of yours, so you can't get me off with him to cover your trail. We're on to you.'

It was all meant as a joke, but as she looked at them, standing side by side and laughing, she suddenly felt shut out and ganged-up-on. She hastily took a large gulp of her drink to prevent herself saying something very stupid and sour which she would have regretted instantly.

CHAPTER FOUR

MILES HAD evidently decided that he was going to enjoy the party at all costs, for he started his first drink at six when Jennie was in the shower, and at seven o'clock when Andrew arrived with the booze in the back of his station-wagon he was wandering up and down the veranda in jeans and a shirt, with his bow tie still untied, a tall glass in his hand, singing Bob Dylan songs in a nasal monotone.

Andrew cocked an expressive eye towards the sound as Jennie went to meet him and help him with the boxes of drinks.

'Am I late?' he asked succinctly.

'No, not at all. He's having a funny twenty-four hours I think. How many boxes are there? I don't think we're going to get much help.'

'That's where you're wrong, *cara sposa*,' Miles said, coming up behind her and making her jump. 'See that, Andrew, old thing—see how she jumps guiltily? I wonder what she has on her mind?'

Jennie looked up at Miles in surprise and thought she saw, just for a second, an expression of almost venomous malice in his eyes.

Keeping an even keel, Andrew said, 'Grab hold of this, will

you, Miles, and I'll take this one. Can you manage those two, Jennie?'

'Of course she can. She may be a literary lightweight, but she's a heavyweight when it comes to manual labour. You had a boyfriend once called Manuel Labour, didn't you, dear?'

'Miles, cut it out,' Jennie said gently, wondering if he was very drunk, or if he was only pretending to be. He seemed to shake off his mood instantly.

'Sorry,' he said, and grabbed the box indicated and set off with it for the veranda. Andrew gave Jennie a glance that might have been either warning or sympathy, and followed him.

By the time the rest of the guests started to arrive just after eight, the three of them, with the help of Sofia and Yannis, had laid out the food and drinks in the cool, parquet-floored drawing room which led off the veranda, and had cleared the space at one end of the long double room for the band, and had set up the chairs for them. Of Bea there was still no sign. She had disappeared into her room at six o'clock when Miles and Jennie had gone to dress, and they hadn't heard a sound from her since other than splashings in the bathroom and the sound of drawers opening and shutting.

'What can she be up to in there for two hours?' Jennie wondered aloud to Miles and Andrew, and the former shrugged.

'I think she means to take us by surprise. Perhaps she's planning something outrageous.'

'Make-up can take a surprisingly long time to put on, I understand,' Andrew said soothingly, and then realising that this might sound like a criticism of Jennie he added, 'Of course, you have such beautiful skin you don't need make-up, so I suppose you wouldn't take that long.'

Jennie smiled her thanks for the rather clumsy compliment, and Miles placed his arm across her shoulders, saying, 'What do you think of her tonight, Andy? Don't you think she's looking exceptionally well?'

Jennie was wearing a lilac-blue crepe dress which showed

off her tan to the best advantage, and which had a close-fitting, low-necked bodice accentuating her good bust, and a full skirt to hide her not-so-good hips. She had thought she looked rather nice. Now Miles had made her feel awkward, and she cursed him inwardly. Andrew muttered something and Miles went on boisterously, 'Come on, old man, you can do better than that. Speak up, let's know what you think of my wife.'

'Jennie knows what I think of her,' Andrew said quietly.

'I don't think she does,' Miles said a little too quickly, resulting in a strained silence. Andrew turned abruptly and went away to the drinks table to refill his glass and regain his composure, and Jennie turned on Miles angrily.

'What the hell's got into you tonight? Will you stop trying to embarrass Andrew? What's he ever done to you? Don't keep pushing me at him that way.'

Miles dropped his hand from her shoulder and stared at her with a curious expression, part contrite, part speculative.

'I just thought you might find solace in each other,' he said.

'Solace for what?'

'For being a failure.'

'I don't feel a failure,' Jennie said. 'You are the one who thinks I am.'

'No, I don't think you are. That's part of the trouble.'

'What trouble? You aren't making sense, Miles.'

'Sorry. Skip it.'

'But—'

'I said skip it. Look, I'm sorry, I'm behaving badly. I'll stop getting at old Toulouse.' Miles called him that because he had two loos, one upstairs and one down.

'Thank you. And please don't call him Toulouse. It's a very worn joke.'

'Hokay, boss. How about another snort?' He held up his hand in the sign of peace, and she placed her hand against it, relieved but still puzzled.

Practically everyone had arrived and the party atmosphere was beginning to warm up and the noise level of the conversations to rise when Bea finally made her appearance, coming in at the end of the long room and causing the conversation to stop dead. Thirty or so middle-aged people in the kind of clothes that had never been fashionable and noticeably amateur haircuts turned their heads and stared. Bea, tall, slim, beautiful, with a glowing golden tan that made her skin look as if it had been polished, stood there in a catsuit made of a material that looked like soft silver paper. In the front was a panel of wide-mesh silver chain mail through which her small breasts and dark nipples were clearly visible. Her feet rested in unbelievably high-heeled sandals, and her finger- and toenails were painted silver too. Her eyes were as blue as fireworks in her brown face, her make-up was immaculate and subtle, and her silver-streaked blonde hair was swept back from her face and hung in a great mane almost to her waist.

In the ensuing silence someone was heard to whisper 'Shit!' in a reverent tone of wonder, and Jennie was stirred from her reverie to go forward and make a rescue—not that Bea looked as if she needed rescuing. She had a closed smile of accomplishment on her lips; if anything, it was the rest of the party who needed rescue. All the male guests were standing up a little straighter and pulling in their stomachs, and all the female guests were watching the males and looking either cross or bemused. Jennie's sense of humour came belatedly to her rescue. In her ancient, old-fashioned, middle-aged frock, designed to show off her hopelessly out-of-date breasts, she hurried across the room and took Bea by the hand and drew her forward, saying,

'Bea, darling, you look absolutely marvellous. Come and meet everybody,' and she fished around in the group nearest her for the best person to start the ball rolling. Her choice fell on James Laurence, a multi-pseudonymed writer who had settled on Crete with his wife Lisa to avoid the unpleasant consequences of his financial success. Jim's sartorial tastes leaned towards what he considered his youthful heyday when he had sat in the back row of the pictures watching James Dean and dreaming of motorbikes, and even on the hottest days he wore a much-studded leather jacket with his jeans and high-heeled cowboy boots, while his quiff and d.a. were always immaculate. If anyone could cope with a semi-naked Bea, it was Jim.

Jennie made the introduction and held her breath. Jim bowed over Bea's hand and said, 'I see you're throwing your guests open to the public, Jen. Any chance of a private viewing?'

'Careful, darling,' Lisa said without malice, 'you're dribbling on her bare skin.'

'Jim's a writer too,' Jennie explained to Bea.

'Oh? What sort of things do you write?' Bea asked politely, attempting to withdraw her hand without making an unseemly fuss.

Jim smiled without ever once taking his eyes from her nipples and said, 'Oh, anything they ask me for—sex books, westerns, science fiction.'

'A veritable hack, like me,' Jennie said.

'But saved from mediocrity by the meaningfulness I manage to inject into my popular prose,' Jim said with assumed dignity.

'Except that no one knows what it's meant to mean,' Lisa put in. Jim smiled sweetly at her.

'Meaningfulness doesn't have to mean anything—as long as it's meaningful.'

'In fact,' Jennie said, 'he sells his copyrights for a pot of message.'

'While you,' Jim countered, 'do it—or I should say, did it —by exposing your cleavage to sensitive editors over lunches.'

'I was a legend in my own lunchtime,' Jennie said.

'That's a steal,' Jim pointed out.

'All things have been said before,' Jennie countered.

'And that's a cop-out.'

'Cop-out! Just listen to you! At least I don't massacre the English language.'

'Only because you never mastered it.'

Lisa put her hand on Bea's arm. 'Once these two get at it,

there's no stopping them. Let me introduce you to some other people.'

'And don't let any other people introduce themselves into her,' Jim added. 'I claim *jus prima nocte.*'

'On what grounds?' Jennie challenged.

'Oh, just outside by the veranda will do, as long as the wife's not looking.'

'You see what I mean?' Lisa said to Bea, and led her away, leaving Jennie smiling happily to herself in the pleasant realisation that Bea hadn't said anything for the last five minutes.

'Datta. Dayadhvam. Damyata,' Jim said, looking at Jennie looking at Bea.

'What's that?'

'What the Thunder Said,' he said. 'The thunder you've just arranged to have stolen, using me, I might add, as Oliver Twist to your Bill Sykes. Next time you want someone to climb in the pantry window, ask Andrew.'

'Can't in this case,' Jennie said.

'Oh, I see. You're aiming that thirty-three-inch gun at poor old Andrew, are you?'

'Poor old Andrew nothing. You said yourself you'd like to see over the building.'

'In my case it's different. I'm not in love with you.'

'Aren't you?'

'Well—not as much as he is, you siren.'

'Talking of which, I'd better get a Doppler shift on, and circulate myself round some more guests. A few of those present are still palpitating from the shock of Bea's exposé.'

'Jennie.' He was suddenly serious, calling her back. She raised an eyebrow enquiringly. 'I would keep an eye on Miles, if I were you. He looks as if he's suffering from shell-shock as well.'

Jennie looked across the room towards the corner where Miles, glass in hand, was chattering with unexpected vivacity to Kay Smithson. His eyes were not on Kay, but looking across her shoulder towards Bea's bare brown back. But then, so was every other male eye in the room.

'Miles?' she said, almost derisively. 'He's safe enough. All he cares about is his book—whichever one he's working on. As long as she doesn't disturb him he ignores her.'

'I think you're wrong,' Jim said carefully. 'At least, it looks to me as if she is disturbing him, quite a bit.'

'Oh phooey,' she said, but kissed his cheek to thank him for his care.

Jim was evidently anxious to look after her interests, however, for not long afterwards in her circulating she discovered Miles bracketed by Jim and Ben Hyssop, a massive, bearded, saturnine writer of crime stories whose reticence about his past had given rise to a lot of surmise about where he got his detailed information on police procedure and prison life. The three of them were talking about royalties, a subject of absorbing interest to all writers, and Jim had manoeuvered Miles into a corner with Ben between him and freedom. Jennie then put the remainder of her plan to work by indicating subtly to Andrew that Bea felt a bit out of things (all appearances to the contrary) and that she needed someone to take care of her. Andrew fell for it. Suggest to him that something would be a kindness, and he'd do it. Offer him the most attractive woman in the room and he'd say it was time he was going.

So when the dance troupe arrived, amid cheers, and the guests cleared the end of the room for them, Jennie saw Bea and Andrew standing together, talking animatedly, and she smiled happily. Andrew, as she knew of her own experience, was a fascinating talker when he got going.

There were six dancers, five men and one woman, and they were dressed in their traditional dancing costumes, black and scarlet and hung all about with thin silver discs that chimed softly as they moved. The men wore their baggy, wrap-around pants with the legs tucked into soft, raw-leather boots, and their shirts hanging open to the waist to show their bare, silky, golden skin. They were typical Cretans, small, supple and rounded in body, with sweet, small-featured faces, fine silky hair the colour of toffee, and wide, honey-hazel eyes as slanting as a wild cat's. Two of them were

Sofia's sons, and they grinned a shy welcome to Jennie and then, at her encouraging nod, came over to shake hands with her before they began their dancing.

The Cretan dancing was unlike peasant dancing that Jennie had seen in other parts of the world. It involved a lot of intricate footwork without much other movement of the body, and the stamping and twirling was oddly muted as if it had evolved in a nation of flat-dwellers. Jennie had at first found it rather somnolent, but custom had lent her interest, and she now enjoyed watching out for particular variations of step, for one step differed from another by so little that to the uninitiated they appeared to be doing the same thing over and over.

Towards the end of the display some of the guests joined in, as was also traditional, and the troupe ran forward to drag unwilling participants into the fray. Jennie was amused to note that by some common consent they did not solicit Bea, and she guessed that their modesty was offended by Bea's naked breasts. Then Sofia's eldest, Giorgiou, ran up and took Jennie's hand, and happily she went with him. She loved this particular dance, which she called to herself The Queen's Delight, because some of its little shuffling, hopping steps reminded her of morris dancing, and she loved dancing with Giorgiou, who combined the lightness of a feather with the springiness of an indiarubber.

This was the last dance, and the musicians played faster and faster, so that the long snake of dancers rocked and swayed round the small space in a perilous way, dropping the unfit or the merely-too-drunk as the pace increased. Then Giorgiou dropped Jennie's hand and ran out in front of them and did his high leaps, flinging himself vertically into the air, drawing up his feet and clapping his hands between and behind them, arching his body in the air like a cat, while his flying necklaces caught the light like spray. The guests cheered him on to higher and higher leaps, and the remainder of the dancers whirled about him until Jennie wondered how she could ever have thought Cretan dancing muted. Then abruptly it was over.

It was always like that. The guests might cheer, applaud, groan or protest, but when Nikos stopped, he stopped, and that was the end. Jennie shook hands with each of the troupe, dancers and musicians, and thanked each of them personally, and they smiled shyly and glanced at each other as if it was the first time they had ever performed. Jennie warmed to them all over again. They were such gentle, modest people. Giorgiou, exceptionally, looked directly into her face, and there was some message for her in his slanting, golden, wild-animal's eyes, but she could not imagine what it was. Then she looked around for Miles, for the money to pay Nikos who would want to go home right away—or rather down to the harbour drink shop.

She could not see him. 'I'm sorry—just a moment, please—I'll have to go and look for him,' she said to the troupe, and edged her way through the guests towards the veranda, guessing he had gone outside. One or two of the party were out there by the rail, looking at the moonlit sea, or not, as the case might be, but not Miles. Giorgiou appeared behind her.

'Nikos say it does not matter,' he said abruptly. 'You give him the moneys some other time, is okay.'

'Nikos said that?' Jennie said in stark disbelief. Giorgiou's golden cheeks darkened with embarrassment, but he nodded all the same. Abruptly cold touched her, and she shivered. 'What is it, Giorgiou?' she asked, but he looked at her enquiringly and without comprehension.

'Is all right,' he said. Jennie shook her head.

'No, I'll find him. He's probably in the loo or something. I'd pay it myself but I used all my cash yesterday buying booze and things, and I know Nikos won't do with a cheque.'

Giorgiou smiled at that. 'Nikos a very fine man, but he can't read. What he do with a cheque?'

'Precisely,' Jennie said, and went back in. She looked around the other rooms, and finally headed for their bedroom, and there at last she found him, coming out and shutting the door behind him firmly.

'Ah, there you are. Have you got the money for Nikos?'

Jennie asked. He looked startled, stared at her as if he did not understand what she was saying. 'The money for the troupe,' she repeated impatiently. His hair and clothes were rumpled, and he looked bleary as if he'd been asleep. Jennie guessed he was drunk. Well, he worked hard enough, he deserved to rest in his own way. Clumsily he dug into his pocket and drew out a handful of notes which he pushed at her. She took them without counting, and then smiled.

'Having a good time, darling?' she said, reaching up to pat his cheek, and to her surprise he flinched from her. She raised an eyebrow and turned away, discovering Giorgiou still behind her and hustling her in a surprising way towards the other door where the troupe waited. Behind her the bedroom door opened again, and she turned her head to look. Giorgiou actually took her elbow to push her onwards, as if afraid she would abscond with the money, but she caught a glimpse all the same of someone coming out of the bedroom who could only, in that outfit, be Bea.

When she had paid off the troupe, Jennie went out on to the veranda and stood alone at the far end looking down to the sea. Giorgiou from the vantage point of one of his leaps must have spotted them going into the bedroom together, and that was why he was so anxious to keep her from looking for Miles. She smiled at the memory. Sweet, kind boy! Well, what of it? Miles, a bit drunk, Bea, a very attractive girl, a couple of kisses in a dark room—nothing to make a fuss about. The Cretans, of course, lived by what seemed for a westerner very remote standards. If a Cretan boy kissed a Cretan girl he had to marry her. She couldn't help being just the tiniest bit hurt, but that was pique, she told herself, nose-out-of-joint stuff. She'd get over it. A movement made her turn her head, and Andrew appeared beside her.

'I'm off, Jennie,' he said.

'Must you?' she said, but it was only out of habit. 'Have you had a good time?'

'Yes. Have you?'

'Strange question. It was my party. Did you like Bea?'

He hesitated. 'I've grown out of touch, I suppose, being here for so long.'

'I know what you mean,' Jennie said. 'I sometimes wonder—'

'It might be good for you,' Andrew said.

'What might?' Jennie said, startled.

'A trip home.'

'How did you know what I was going to say?'

'Of course I knew,' Andrew said seriously. 'I love you—I know everything about you.' He had never actually said it before. Jennie looked at him in distress.

'Oh, Andrew—'

'It's all right,' he said, smiling ruefully. 'It isn't anything you need to worry about. I've lived with it for so long now it's just part of the background, it doesn't hurt or anything. But I just thought you might like to know. Does that publisher still want you to make a publicity tour?'

'You are being cryptic tonight,' Jennie said, smiling.

'Too much to drink. Too much moonlight.'

'Moonlight can be cruelly deceptive, Amanda,' she said.

'And human kind cannot bear too much reality,' he counter-quoted. 'I really have had too much to drink. Goodnight, princess, and flights of angels sing thee to thy rest. Come and see me soon.'

'I will. Goodnight, Andrew.'

Jim Laurence was next. 'I'm giving Ben a lift, so you needn't worry about him,' he said. 'Good party, love. I always like coming here. Lisa and I must have another one soon. We seem to be bumming everywhere these days, but you know what it's like when you have kids.'

'Well, no, I don't actually.'

'No, of course you don't. Silly of me. Listen, if you want to get rid of your house guest, send her on to me. I'll call it research and have her taken off my tax as an expense. I might even get her clothes taken off as well.'

'Not a doubt in the world,' Jennie laughed. 'But what would Lisa say?'

'It was Lisa's idea.'

'Then you really are in trouble,' Jennie said. She reached up to kiss him, and he folded both arms round her and pressed her hard and briefly against his Hells Angels jacket.

'I'll risk it,' he said. 'Take care, love, won't you?'

When the last guest had gone, Jennie went back out on to the veranda, kicked off her shoes, and drew a chair up so that she could sit and rest her feet on the rail. The moon had gone down, and the sea was dark and quiet in the scented blackness below them. Bea came wandering out, yawning noisily.

'Should we clear up, or something?'

'I never do,' Jennie said. 'Sofia will make a start in the morning, and we can help her then. Takes the shine off a party to clear up right away, I always think.'

'Hm,' Bea said, and came to lean on the rail beside her. Her hair was tangled and her make-up smudged.

'You look as though you've had a good time, Bacchante,' Jennie said.

'Oh, I did,' Bea said. She didn't look at Jennie. Her eyes were half-closed, languorously.

'What did you think of the dancers?' Jennie tried next. Bea smiled a little and licked her lips.

'Lovely,' she said. 'Those Cretan boys—what lollipops! I think I'll take a couple home with me, in my suitcase; I could fancy having a couple of them around the flat to draw my bath and bring me tall glasses of sherbet and rub oil into my back. I wonder if you'd have to declare them at Customs?'

'They are dutiable,' Jennie said. 'Anyway, if anyone's going to take them back to England, it'll be me—I saw them first.'

Now Bea did look, one quick glance, and she said, 'Are you thinking of going back to England, then?'

Jennie paused before answering, and Bea studied her long silver fingernails. 'I might,' she said at last. 'Just for a visit. I miss the old country, and you've brought me the realisation of how far down a backwater we are here. The main flow of life is passing me by. England must have changed so much since I've been away.'

'I love the quietness here,' Bea said. 'I'm so sick of

competition and grub, grub, grub and all the in-fighting and bitchiness. It's so simple here. Clean air and clear values.'

Jennie raised an eyebrow. 'I'm not so sure about the values. I imagine they're the same everywhere. But, plain and simply, I'm homesick. I've been homesick for five years without realising it.'

'Will you go back, then?' Bea asked in a small voice.

'Oh, I haven't got as far as that yet,' Jennie said. 'But perhaps I might fly back when you go, just for a visit.'

Bea said, 'I—'

'Yes?'

'Oh, nothing. Jen, I don't much want to go back. I think I'd like to stay.'

'Well, you'd easily enough get a job. Courier or guide. Or the Smithsons would give you a job in their hotel. It's called the Hotel Asterion, but we call it Hotel Akrivo. That's a joke—in Cretan akrivo means Bloody Expensive. Or Andrew would find you something. I think he'd like an assistant in his shop, so that he could take time off to do more painting. You like Andrew, don't you?'

'He's nice,' Bea said, but her mind was far away.

'Or, of course,' Jennie went on, not knowing quite why she was saying it, 'I'm sure Jim Laurence would take you on as his mistress.'

Bea looked round at that, sharply, and in the light from the windows Jennie saw she looked both hurt and apprehensive.

'I'm sorry,' Jennie said. 'It wasn't much of a joke, was it? I'm a little tired. Not used to all this jollity, you see. I think I'd better go to bed.'

She got up, and Bea's eyes followed her anxiously.

'Jen—' she said suddenly. Jennie waited, but did not turn, and after a moment Bea simply said, 'Goodnight.'

'Goodnight, Bea darling. Sweet dreams.'

CHAPTER FIVE

SOMETHING WAS going wrong. Miles seemed more than usually bad-tempered, and seemed to find it hard to say a civil word to Jennie. He did not make love to her, and when she tried to tempt him he pushed her away irritably but without saying why he didn't want her. When she asked him if his work was going badly, he snapped, 'Of course it's bloody well going badly. What kind of a stupid question is that?'

'A civil question,' she said quietly. 'I should have thought it deserved a civil answer at least.'

'The day *you* think—' he growled.

'Is Bea disturbing you?' Jennie persevered. 'I can get rid of her if she is. She needn't be inconvenienced—she could stay down in the village.'

'Oh, for God's sake!' Miles said abruptly. 'Grow up!' and he turned and stalked away without further explanation.

Worse—or, well, perhaps not actually worse, but as bad anyway—her own work was suffering. She could not concentrate. She would sit down every morning at her typewriter, and the words, instead of flowing in their usual happy way, stuck in her brain like hairballs. She had always, all her life, been able to forget everything when she sat down to write. The act of writing, of creating even in the small and unimportant way she created, had washed all awareness of trouble and unhappiness from her, and the flow of words from her on to paper had always both soothed and stimulated her.

Now she felt faintly nauseated at the thought of another three thousand words to be put down before she could in conscience get up again from her typewriter and do other things. Her typing grew erratic in the extreme, littered with unwanted fractions and capital letters, and when she hit the p instead of the o for the fourth time in the same line, she gave up in despair. She was far enough ahead of schedule for it not to matter too much if she did not do her three thousand words for one day.

But stopping work was as bad as trying to start. She was restless and miserable, without precisely knowing why, and while she felt she could not work, she did not want to do anything else. Outside the sun shone down from a blue sky, but the sun seemed tiring and the sky brassy. She did not want to swim or sunbathe or walk or read or listen to music. She wanted company, but the thought of finding someone and talking to them sickened her. She wanted to work, but she couldn't bring herself to do it.

My God, she thought, perhaps I'm really blocked. The lurking horror that attacks writers in the middle of the night after a late supper with too much garlic attacked her in broad daylight: perhaps I'll never write again! Perhaps the gift—the inexplicable and unendingly delightful ability to write—had deserted her. She had lost it, and she had nothing more to say, she would never write another word, she would have to go and be a sales assistant or a computer programmer or something equally horrific! In terror she turned again to her typewriter, and finding it still impossible she assuaged her guilt and fear by finishing reading the proofs that had been hanging around for far too long, and then, feeling better, she turned to her accounts, which ought to have been done long since too, and so the morning passed.

The atmosphere in the villa was tense, but it always improved after dark, when they had had dinner and the three of them relaxed in enormous squashy chairs on the veranda.

Miles and Jennie, both a little bruised though for, apparently, different reasons, stretched out and were silent, and Bea, fresh and glowing and wearing each day some outfit more daring, attractive and original than the day before, would read to them from *Winnie the Pooh* or *The Wind in the Willows* or *The Tailor of Gloucester.* It was as if they were invalids, convalescing from some sickness both shocking and weakening. Bea came between them and their wounds like a palliative, like a balm. Sometimes she sang to them, and sometimes she talked to them, but mostly she read from books with simple, tested magic, which bound them all together, but kept them carefully from touching, like the crumpled tissue paper that keeps stored apples apart.

When Bea had been there a month, she began on *Watership Down*, and in the sweet, scented night, safe, she thought, in the darkness, Jennie began to cry.

Bea read on as if she had not noticed, but after a while Miles got up explosively from his chair and said, 'Oh, for God's sake, we can't go on like this!'

Bea's voice faltered and stopped, and Jennie held her breath, not wanting to cry without the cover of sound. She gave one convulsive sob, and the noise of it, too loud in the silence, shocked her out of her crying.

'We're going to have to talk,' Miles said. He sounded angry, and he walked up and down the veranda not looking at either of them. Jennie, avoiding Bea's eye, watched him, and saw with a sense of shock that he was not angry. His anger she was used to, and could cope with, because in a sense it was nothing to do with her but was an expression of something inside him that was directed towards himself. But what she saw in his face was not anger. She knew, with a sickening apprehension, that she was about to be hurt. It was like the split second before a car crash, when you know it is going to happen.

'I don't want to,' she said desperately.

'Are you working?' he swung round to her accusingly. 'No,' he answered for her. 'And neither am I. Do you know how many words I've done in this last week? I'll tell you. I've written nothing. I've torn up two-thirds of a chapter. That's a score of minus five thousand words. Not bad for a week's work, eh? At that rate, I can have unwritten *War and Peace* by the time I'm fifty.'

'It isn't my fault,' Jennie began automatically. Miles clasped his brow melodramatically—but, she thought, amazingly calmly, he had always taken himself very seriously.

'Jesus Christ, Jennie, who said it was? Don't you realise what's going on? Don't you realise we've reached a crisis? We've got to get it all out in the open.'

'Go on then,' Bea said soothingly. 'You talk. We'll listen.'

Lack of opposition stymied him. He was silent, and walked up and down a couple more times. Bea was looking at Jennie, anxiously, but Jennie still avoided her eye. One did not court the pain of accident.

At last, calmer, Miles stopped before the two women and said in a gentler voice, 'Jennie, I never thought I'd have to say this, but I've fallen in love with another woman.'

There, it was said. The words, trite and hackneyed as they were from a hundred films and books, hurt with the freshness of a newly-honed knife. Although she had known he was going to say it, she still felt herself jar with the shock, felt herself begin to tremble from it. The amazing thing about reality is how real it really is.

'I don't want to hurt you,' he went on. 'God knows, I never wanted to hurt you, but it's just one of those things. It happens, and there's nothing anyone can do.'

Jennie's mind rejected all of those statements, but she heard herself say all the same, reading from the same script, 'What did I do wrong?'

He flung himself on his knees in front of her, and said with genuine feeling, 'Nothing! It was nothing you did or didn't do!' She was amazed that he did not know she had only said the words for something to say. Did he really think she was that idiotic, or had that low an opinion of herself? In the midst of her pain she continued to think calmly, and wonder how it was that men were so much more susceptible to cliché than women. He was still talking. 'I loved you—I still love you in one way. You've been a wonderful wife to me, but I've fallen in love with someone else. It isn't that I don't love you—it's just that I love her more. I'm so sorry, Jennie, truly I am.'

'You're not,' she heard herself say. It gave him pause, and then he got to his feet, dignity wounded.

'All right,' he said coldly, 'I'm not. Have it your own way.'

She was sorry to have alienated him—bad enough to have this happening without his hostility—but she recognised he was manoeuvring her, even at this late stage. If he could make her hostile, it would be easier for him. She hated him at that moment, and her anger mounted in spite of herself.

'Have it my way? What the hell do you mean, have it my way? I have to have it your way, like it or not, don't I? What am I supposed to do, fall on my knees in gratitude because you're *sorry* you're doing this? You want *thanks*?'

That was better. He could look noble and forgive her now. 'I can understand you being angry,' he said.

'*Your* being angry,' she corrected him maliciously. 'Being is a verbal substantive and takes a possessive.' He looked nobler still.

'Go ahead. Yell at me. Hit me if you like. I deserve it.'

'You are the worst fucking hypocrite I've ever met in my life,' Jennie screamed, beside herself, temporarily, with rage. 'You don't think you deserve it at all. You just want me to punish you by being angry so you won't feel so guilty. Jesus Christ, you bastard, you not only want to leave me for another woman, you want me to make it easy for you as well!' This was getting her nowhere. She controlled herself abruptly and said as calmly as if nothing had happened, 'Well, I'm not playing. I'm going to be as sweet and reasonable as I've always been. If you want to do this, you do it on your own responsibility. I wish there was some way I could make sure you'd really feel it as you do it, but knowing your powers of self-deception you'll find some way of blocking out the reality from your psyche as soon as it starts to hurt.'

She stopped, and there was silence. Miles was staring at her, and just for one rewarding second he looked ashamed, before he covered it up. It was his way, when something happened he didn't like, to rewrite the story in his head to make it go the way he wanted. She knew—wasn't she a writer too? Endless versions passed and repassed, until at last you couldn't be sure which one had actually happened and which you had made up. And in some senses, all of them had, and none of them had. What was reality, after all? It was all in the mind. At last she said, 'You wanted to talk—then talk.'

'I don't know what to say,' he said. 'I don't want to provoke another outburst.'

'Well it seems to me you've omitted one important formality. You haven't asked the lady in question what she feels about it.'

They both looked at Bea, who had been making herself very small in her chair up to now, as one does when finding oneself trapped too close to a dog-fight. She looked once, significantly, into Miles's eyes, and then addressed herself to Jennie.

'I'm sorry, Jen, but I'm in love with Miles. I wish it hadn't happened, but it has, and I'm too selfish to be noble about it. If he loves me, there's no sense in two of us being unhappy, is there?'

'The classic argument,' Jennie said, but without hostility. Unlike Miles, Bea genuinely was sorry, and Jennie accepted the honesty of her answers. 'Well, what are we going to do?' No one, of course, answered that. Jennie tried again, being more specific, looking at Miles. 'What do you want to do?'

'I don't know,' he said evasively. 'I am in love with Bea. If she loves me—'

'We've done that bit,' Jennie said impatiently. 'Do you want to divorce me?'

The word had been said; there was no going back now; but Jennie had no more sense of frontier than if she had passed a milestone in a high-speed train. Miles and Bea looked at each other, and that was what hurt. Already there was a complicity between them that made Jennie the outsider. *They* were the couple now: how quickly it could happen, as quickly as one sentence. She knew then what she must do, but she said nothing.

Bea still kept resolutely silent, so it had to be Miles who spoke. Good for you, Bea, Jennie thought. Make him commit himself.

'I want to marry Bea,' he said at last. 'So, I suppose, that means we would have to get divorced.' Jennie looked at him steadily, without comment, and he went on, 'Would you stand in our way? I mean, would you contend it?'

'What grounds are you thinking of using?' she asked. Bea now took the reins.

'We've already provided grounds,' she said quietly. Jennie cursed herself for feeling shocked. Of course they have, idiot, she chided herself. Did you think they held hands and talked about poetry?

'Where?' she asked. 'When?'

'For God's sake,' Miles protested, but Bea knew better than to think it was morbid curiosity.

'More than once,' she said. 'During the mornings, while you were working, sometimes we went down to the beach, or for walks.'

Jennie stood up and turned away from them, sickened. *That* was shock, of course, for there was nothing intrinsically shocking in it. She looked down at the dark sea, and felt the cool night air blowing against her face. I shall miss this place, she thought, and then voiced the thought's logical precursor.

'I want to go home.' Home to England, cool, green England, lush and rich and wooded. How she missed softly rounded hills, watermeadows, lanes like green tunnels, bluebell woods, tender grey skies, the subtle shades and smells that Crete, brassily beautiful as it was, could never offer. 'I won't make difficulties for you—what would be the point? Firmans want me to do a publicity tour. I'll write to Maurice and he can arrange everything, and when it's over, I'll stay there. You can get the divorce any way you like, as long as you don't bother me with it. I don't want anything from you, Miles, no alimony or anything like that. I'll support myself just as I've always done.' She glanced behind her. Miles was standing beside Bea now, his hand on her shoulder, and Bea's hand on his. Her husband! A stranger now, and Jennie was no longer, would never again be, entitled to touch him or know what he was thinking. The first cold weight of loneliness settled in her chest like an inverse heartburn.

'I'm not entirely envious of you, Bea. Once an animal has tasted blood—' Bea understood, as Jennie knew she would. But she had no spleen against Bea. She looked at Miles. 'Was it because I was a writer too?'

'In part,' he admitted, with unwonted honesty. 'You should know, we can never bear competition. You never admired me enough.'

'Nor you me,' Jennie said. Miles took it as the words of his release.

'Then it's all right, isn't it?'

'Oh, no,' Jennie smiled sourly. 'I won't give you that. The best you can hope for out of this match is a draw.'

It was typical of Miles that, having won what he wanted to win, he was in no hurry to take it, and would have allowed the situation at the villa to drift on after that day almost indefinitely, with his new love and his old around him while he worked and took his pleasure. Bea was thoroughly unhappy, and perversely, now it was possible and to an extent permissible, would not have sex with Miles as long as Jennie was living there. And Jennie, as was equally typical of her, wanted everything settled at once. She moved into a spare bedroom that first night, and spent the hours she could not sleep writing to Maurice, telling him as much of the story as she felt he needed to know to convince him of the urgency of the case, and also to Angus Mitchell of Firman and Jackson. She told him only that she wanted a trip home and would agree to a publicity tour. Maurice would tell him, in absolute confidence, the circumstances, which would make sure he knew without Jennie having to commit the indelicacy of telling him.

She remained at the villa only one day more, to pack and to explain to Sofia and Yannis, and then she moved down into the village to stay with Andrew. Miles's eyes lit up with relief when she told him where she was going, but she soon disabused him of the idea.

'You'd like it if I had an affair with Andrew, wouldn't you? It would relieve you of the responsibility. Well, tough luck, buddy, I'm not that way inclined. I like Andrew, as I always have, and that's all.'

'You may surprise yourself one day.'

'Oh, no. I shall never be surprised by my own feelings. You've avoided responsibility all your life, Miles, but it's only responsibility that makes a man of a boy.'

Miles's mouth turned down sourly. 'Your own nobility is beginning to go to your head. You're starting to talk like the Reader's Digest Points To Ponder. I hope you're writing down all these truths for posterity—it would be terrible for them to be lost.'

'Stick your head up your arse, Egerton,' she said pleasantly. There was no answer to that.

Andrew was a good person to spend the next few weeks with, showing his sympathy only by not asking her anything, and by listening without comment when she felt the need to talk. It helped her to talk through the situation, fixing it for herself in the way it was, rather than the more pleasant but dangerous Way She Would Have Liked It To Be which she would eventually have ended up believing had she had no one to talk to. Bea had come to the villa predisposed to like Miles, because she admired his work, and perhaps predisposed by her image of the kind of life they led there to fall in love, it didn't matter with whom.

'I hoped she'd fall in love with you,' Jennie admitted shamefaced to Andrew as they sat by the open window of his sitting room one evening. 'I've suffered Emma Woodhouse's fate in a way, haven't I, through attempting to matchmake.'

'You didn't push very hard,' Andrew comforted her. 'And

judging by the time interval whatever happened between them must have happened almost at first sight.'

'That day I came down here to arrange the party—when I got back they'd gone swimming together. He would never break off his work period for anything. I suppose you're right. He was already in love with her. I wonder I didn't spot it sooner. Even after the party I thought there was nothing in it, despite Giorgiou's warning.'

'Giorgiou?'

'He must have seen them go into the bedroom together. He tried to shield me. And,' she remembered, 'Jim Laurence offered to take Bea off my hands. He must have noticed something too. Everyone,' she shook her head sadly, 'but me. Am I naïve?'

'Naïve perhaps isn't the word for it. Innocent, maybe.'

'Stupid,' Jennie said dully.

'Trusting. Innocent and trusting.'

'It certainly sounds better,' she conceded, 'but after all, I am supposed to be a novelist. I write all the time about human relationships, love and romance, all that kind of caper.' She sighed. 'I suppose the thing is, it was all so different in the past, and I write mostly historical romance. I've been brain-washed by my own fiction. An appropriate fate, I suppose. If you listen very carefully, you will hear the gods laughing.'

Andrew said nothing, but his eyes remained on her steadily and sympathetically.

After a while she went on, 'It was perhaps never a good thing for us to marry, two writers. I've seen marriages break up before, between musicians and between actors. Perhaps it's a universal rule that artists of any sort should never marry each other. But I thought we were happy. Not ecstatically so, but happy enough. And who needs ecstasy?'

'Should you settle for less?' Andrew asked quietly. She considered.

'I've never believed it possible. I always thought I was being level-headed and sensible not to expect too much out of life. But, after all, perhaps—'

'One never gets all one expects,' Andrew said. 'So if you expect less, you probably end up getting less.'

'The corollary being, expect everything and you might end up with enough.' He assented to the proposition. 'I was happy enough with him, though. I admired his work.'

'But not in the way he wanted. You admired him as a technician. You read him as a writer and not as a reader.'

'That's true, but what else could he expect? I am a writer. I can't change that.'

'You should know what he wanted. You've always told me that writers thrive on admiration and flattery, the grosser the better. What did you want from him?'

Jennie considered, and then said, her surprise apparent in her voice, 'Nothing. I didn't want anything from him, as far as my writing went. It functioned in a separate sort of sphere. I didn't care whether he admired or praised my work or not. I didn't care—' She paused and then went on, more surprised than ever: 'I didn't care for his opinion at all.'

Andrew left her to work out the moral of that for a while, and then said, 'I think perhaps you will find you miss him rather less than you expect.'

Jennie shook her head. 'I did love him, Andrew. I *do* love him. I'm going to miss him horribly. And it's always a blow to the ego, to be rejected.'

'I know,' he said kindly. 'You'll suffer, but in the end you'll be better off.'

'Now don't tell me I'll be better off without him. People always say that. It just isn't true. Our marriage may not have been perfect, but I'd sooner have had it than not have it.'

'That, ultimately, isn't the choice you have to make. The question is not would you rather have Miles than no one. The question is, would you rather have Miles than anyone else.'

Jennie spread her hands. 'How can I tell? I haven't met anyone else.'

'Precisely. Jennie, darling, I'm going to give you a piece of advice. You'll find, as a potential divorcee, that everyone will give you advice, unsolicited and mostly useless, but mine will be unique and very useful if you can remember to follow it.'

Jennie smiled for the first time that evening. 'Tell me, then. I'm listening.'

'You'll have offers, plenty of them, and you'll want to take them all. You'll be lonely, and as you said, your ego's taken a bashing. You'll want a few scalps as trophies to prove to yourself you can do it.'

'Lovely picture you're painting of me.'

Andrew ignored the interruption. 'But don't rush into anything. Take your time, don't commit yourself, look around, be choosy. You compromised once, with Miles. Maybe you didn't know in the first place it was a compromise —or maybe you did. You said that you were level-headed about Miles, that you didn't expect ecstasy: that was a compromise. Don't compromise again. Expect everything, don't settle for less than a hundred per cent. You have absolutely nothing to lose, so play for the highest possible stakes.'

'Go for broke, eh?' Jennie said. She looked at Andrew with sudden, sharp sympathy. What an extraordinary man he was! Here she was, facing divorce and running to him for comfort, to the person who, however seriously, had told her he loved her. It was his chance to win her, if he wanted to— she knew how easy it would be for her to succumb to comfort and kindness—but what did he do? He gave her advice which, if she took it, would ensure that he lost her for ever. Either that was courage, or it was crazy. He met her eyes, and she saw it was courage. She reached across and took his hand.

'You're too good to me, 'Drew. I don't know why.'

'You will, one day. If you take my advice, one day you'll meet someone who means to you what you mean to me, and then you'll know it isn't really being good. There's nothing else one can do.'

She was caught wrong-footed. She squeezed his hand, not knowing quite what to say.

'Andrew, I'm sorry,' she said at last.

'Why should you be?'

'I probably haven't made it any easier for you, all these years. But I didn't realise—'

'I know. As I've said, there's a kind of innocence about you, for all that you're so smart. You've got a complicated, subtle brain, Jennie, but about some things you've got a sort of crazy, straightforward simplicity that could be one of your main strengths as well as one of your weaknesses. I suggest you give it full rein. Don't try to muffle it with sophistication. It will tell you when the real thing comes along. And, as I said, don't settle for less than absolutely everything.'

'Including the ecstasy?'

'Definitely including the ecstasy.'

She let him draw her from the chair to his lap. He put his arms round her and then she began to cry, and feeling, even through tears, like someone kicking a dog, she let herself take comfort from him, weeping on his shoulder while he held her and stroked her head as gently and impersonally as if he were not longing all the while to be doing something quite different.

And then, when she had cried enough, he put her to bed in his own bed, tucked her in like a mother, and then went to sleep on the put-you-up in the other room which had been made up for her. It was, she thought drowsily to herself, probably Andrew's Finest Hour.

CHAPTER SIX

THAT COOL, lush, grey-skied England didn't seem so welcoming when Jennie arrived at Heathrow on an Olympic flight one wet day in June. She had forgotten in the interim how sunshine makes everything seem cleaner and prettier, and how, conversely, any air terminus in the rain is sleazy and depressing. Heathrow was full of foreigners. Passengers and those meeting passengers shoved each other around with panicky rudeness, while the staff of the terminus, mainly depressed and emaciated Asians, pushed brooms around lethargically, or wiped filthy tables with dingy clothes that might, to judge from their faces, have originally been wet with their tears.

The grey skies and the grey buildings seemed utterly fantastic when only a few hours before she had left the burning blue sky and blinding sunshine of Crete. The only thing that seemed familiar to her as she walked between the barriers of the arrival hall was that no one around her was speaking English. She was carrying a small overnight bag which contained immediate necessities such as washing-bag and towel and clean underwear and three books—she could never have travelled a mile without a book, even if it was only to the shops. The rest of her luggage, two suitcases, contained little in the way of clothes. The things in the end she had decided to bring away with her from her old life were papers, letters, manuscripts, notebooks. Having looked through the clothes in her wardrobe she had decided that there was nothing there she wouldn't rather replace when she got to England.

For a time she had been eager to bring her typewriter with her—she regarded it, as Miles did his own, like a friend—but common sense had told her in the end that she could buy a new one with less trouble than transporting the old one, even if it were likely to survive a passenger air trip intact. In the end Miles had bought it from her. Jennie had a couple of thousand pounds in a savings account—they had never, thanks to Crete, lived up to their income—and Miles was giving her some more, a lump sum to make up for his keeping the house. At first she had demurred about that, but Andrew and Miles together had gently talked her into it.

'You'll need money for a deposit when you buy your own place in England,' Andrew had pointed out.

'I don't care about a place to live,' Jennie had said sullenly.

'Maybe not, but you will.'

Miles had been more direct.

'Don't be an ass,' he said. 'I have to give you some money.'

'To salve your conscience?' she had asked nastily. Miles took it rather well.

'It's nothing to do with feelings,' he had said gently. 'It's a simple matter of justice. We own this villa together. We've always paid half of all the bills. Therefore in plain equity you have a right to half the value of the place. I haven't got that much now, but I'll give you what I have and the rest later, when I can raise it.'

Jennie had been on the point of saying he could forget the rest but some financial instinct deeper than hurt stopped her. One day, she thought, she might be glad of a debt like that.

So she arrived in England without any immediate financial problems. She arrived, it seemed to her, without anything.

She felt, as amputees are said to feel, as though Miles were still attached to her in some way, itching, but beyond reach of scratching. On the other hand, she felt so scraped out inside she was positively sick. She had refused everything offered on the plane, and still the mere thought of food or drink nauseated her. She had lost everything. She had been wrenched away from her whole life of five years' standing, and the featurelessness of the future she faced filled her with despairing terror. She brought away with her, to make it worse, the knowledge that Miles was already regretting his precipitance. Miles-like, he no sooner discovered himself possessed of the alternative than he wanted to go back to the safety of the relationship he knew. It wasn't, she heard him, with incredulity, say, that he didn't love Bea—it was that he loved Jennie more. If anything had decided Jennie finally that she must leave, it was that. Miles was only one step away from proposing a *ménage à trois.*

Jennie reached the end of the barrier and looked around for Maurice. She had arranged for him to meet her at Heathrow and take her to an hotel, which she had asked him to book for her, but there was no sign of him. Her heart sank the last half-inch and grounded. What was she to do? Telephone, she supposed, to his office. But no, it was nearly six o'clock—there would be no one there. Perhaps he was on his way, held up by traffic or something. She would just have to hang around here.

The arrivals behind her were shoving her painfully in the back as she hesitated and slowed down, and she was looking for somewhere out of the main flow where she could park herself and her luggage trolley when, O joy O bliss, she heard her name called.

'Jennie! Jennie Savage!'

It wasn't Maurice's voice, but it was easy enough to locate. Its owner was swimming against the stream towards her with the ease of a grizzly bear in a bath-tub and before she had had time to speak or even begin to smile her hand was engulfed in two massive paws the size of hams and her face immersed in a hugely-bearded kiss.

'Wonderful to see you, Jennie. Sorry if I'm a bit late—forgot what time you were arriving and had to phone my secretary to ask. How was the trip? Lousy? Always is, isn't it? I hate planes. And of course you must be feeling absolutely bloody. If I'd been you I'd have got utterly pissed and stayed that way. Want a drink here or shall we head for a filling station somewhere? Airports are ghastly, aren't they—make one want to jump in front of a plane, though knowing my luck I'd miss all three wheels and end up with mud on my suit. Is this all your luggage? Shall we have one here, just to keep body and soul apart? Oh Christ, look, don't cry, please, or someone will arrest me. Honestly officer, I wasn't doing anything to her. See him believing that? Come on, look, there's a bar over there. I think you need a bloody enormous Scotch. You're shaking.'

'I think I need one,' Jennie said, the first words she had had a chance to say. 'I'm only crying because it's so nice to see you. What are you doing here?'

'I got wind you were coming and asked Maurice if I could meet you instead of him. He didn't mind—you know Maurice.'

'Yes, quite well actually. He's my agent.'

'So here I am. God, you look marvellous—apart from looking so lousy, I mean. And here we are. Sit down here while I get you something. Scotch?'

'Thanks, Quin.'

He paused on his way from her to smile. 'No one calls me that now, except you and Jim Laurence.'

'He'd have sent his love if he'd known you were going to be here,' Jennie said. Already feeling warm and wanted, she watched Mick West thrust his way through to the bar. He was huge, nearly six feet five, and built like a rugger player, with a great mane of red-gold hair and a huge fiery beard, resembling in Jennie's opinion a young Henry VIII. He and Jim Laurence had worked together in the dim and distant past, and Jim had nicknamed him the Man-Mountain, after Gulliver, which in Lilliputian was Quinbus Flestrin—Quin for short. He was the chief editor at Martin Mandersons, who had published a series of Regency romances by Jennie under a pen-name, Angela Wylde.

When he came back with the Scotch—it looked like at least a treble—and a pint of beer for himself, he sat down opposite her with the care of a man used to breaking chairs and smiled.

'Throw half of that down, and then you'll feel better. You've been crying on the plane. Won't do, you know. If you're going to do a publicity tour, you've got to look your best.'

'Publicity tour?' Jennie asked quizzically. She felt a twinge of apprehension at the thought that perhaps he had the wrong end of the stick. He grinned, and his Scots accent broadened.

'No need to be coy with me, hen. Ye olde magic grapevine is seething. Of course you're going to do a publicity tour. The question is, for whom?'

Jennie opened her mouth to answer but he forestalled her.

'No, don't say it. Maurice told me all. But after all, you write for us too. Why should bloody old Firmans have you? They won't make the best use of you anyway. Old-fashioned outfit. No imagination. Now, if you let me handle you—'

Jennie pretended to misunderstand. 'Oh, is that what you're after? Sleeping your way to the top, eh?'

'You'll never recognise yourself.'

'That's what I'm afraid of. You'd have me do a strip in Princes Street to draw a crowd.'

'It's a thought,' Quin said. 'But listen, Jen, if you go around with old Aberdeen Angus's mob now as Jennie Savage, you can't come round with us later as Angela Wylde. And after all, we had you first. Where's your sense of loyalty?'

'Firmans have been asking me to do a tour for years.'

'Well, so have we. Well, I mean we would have liked you to, but—'

'You've only just thought of it,' Jennie said drily. He shrugged.

'So we've only just thought of it.'

'Anyway, Quin, I've got nearly two new books a year

coming out with Firmans. With you I've only got the four on the backlist.'

He looked eager, and leaned forward so that the small round table rocked alarmingly. 'That's what I wanted to talk to you about. You see, we're going to reissue the Regencies with brand new selling covers, and we want you to do another three new ones as well. We're expanding that part of our list, and we want you at the top of it, that's why we want you to do a promo. In the autumn. So you see, you can't go off on a jaunt with that lot. Have you ever met Angus Mitchell?'

Jennie shook her head. 'He took over after I'd left the country,' she said.

Quin nodded. 'I thought so. Only a person who'd never met him could want to have anything to do with him.'

'You know him?'

He rolled his eyes. 'Do I know him? Remember where I come from. I worked for McKenzies, and I watched him come up. Who could like a man like him?'

'I don't know,' Jennie pointed out patiently. 'I've never met him.'

'You will. And when you do . . . Listen, Jen, I'm not going to bully you on your first evening. I expect you're feeling like a piece of shit at the moment. I'm just asking you not to commit yourself too quickly. Think about it. We want you as much as they do.'

'Nice to know someone wants me,' Jennie muttered, and was instantly sorry. It was an underhand trick to bring her personal circumstances into what, after all, was a business discussion. Quin straightened and smiled sympathetically at her.

'Poor old kid. Never mind, look on the bright side. At least you can write a book about it. If it was me, there'd be nothing on the plus side.'

Jennie smiled tiredly. 'I suppose you're right. A writer's life is like a French cook's stockpot—everything that goes in comes out as nourishing stock.'

'And talking of nourishment—I'm going to take you back to your hotel, and you're going to have a wash and brush up, and then I'm going to take you out for the best meal and bottle of bloody old burgundy we can find. And then we'll tear old Egerton apart, verbally, and that'll make you feel better.'

'Hm. I haven't been feeling savage at all recently,' Jennie murmured wickedly.

'That's my girl,' he said. 'Come on, give me the cases.'

Maurice had booked her into a residential hotel in Bloomsbury at her own request, for she thought she'd feel better in a part of London she knew, and also it was handy for the Piccadilly–Leicester Square area where so many of the publishers seemed to hang out. The room, when she was shown up to it with Quin behind her carrying her bags, was a far more expensive one than she had asked for, and she questioned the booking, but Quin cut her short.

'It's all right—compliments of Mandersons. Can't have our favourite author in a fourth floor back dungeon overlooking the dustbins.'

'How can a dungeon be on the fourth floor?' she asked. 'Quin, this, and the meal—is it bribery? You want me to feel bad?'

Quin patted her head. 'Leave the worrying to me, hen. Listen, I'm doing this for a friend, that's all. How could I ever face Jim Laurence again if I didn't take care of you on your first evening?'

'All right,' Jennie said. 'But tomorrow I'm changing rooms to the one I originally wanted, because from tomorrow I'm paying the bill.'

'I'm glad you realised that,' he grinned. 'Come on, let's go and fold a couple of chops into the system. Any idea where you'd like to go?'

'Bertorellis,' she said without much hesitation. 'That was the first place you ever took me for a publisher's lunch.'

'Was it? I must have been mad. Come on then—we can walk it, if you like, and you can get an idea of what's happened to London since you've been away. And when you've seen that, your own troubles will pale into insignificance.'

Maurice telephoned Jennie at the hotel the next morning, just after—fortunately for their future relationship—she had woken up. He was a small, brisk, dapper man, and his voice over the telephone sounded small, brisk and dapper too. He never wasted any time in introductions, always assuming, when he spoke to her, that she would know who it was. In England, when she was expecting him, this wasn't difficult, but on the few occasions when he had telephoned her in Crete, muffled and distorted by the international cables, it had invariably caused confusion.

'How did you get on last night, then?'

'You might have warned me, Maurice. Better still, you might have met me as promised and let him inveigle me some other way. How did you know I wasn't going to arrive in tears and utterly unseeable.'

'My business as your agent is to bring you together with your publishers, not stand in their way,' he said. 'Anyway, it was better for me—I had some very important telephoning to do.'

'In the evening?'

'Overseas calls,' he said with faint triumph. 'And better for you. You get on far better with him than I do.'

'Everyone gets on with Quin.'

'Yes, but I haven't got your figure. Did he tell you about the reprinting?'

'Yes.'

'Good news, isn't it?'

'I suppose so. And he wants me to write some more. A new contract for three more of the same.'

'He didn't mention that to me,' Maurice said, and she heard the excitement in his voice at the word 'contract'. 'You see, you did yourself a piece of good.'

'I don't know that I want to do them.'

'Of course you do. Don't be ridiculous.'

'I'm not,' Jennie said, resenting the implication. 'I'm just wondering when I'd have the time.'

'He'll wait,' Maurice advised. 'If they're reprinting the old ones he'll wait for the new ones. Don't turn anything down, my darling. Remember you're in England now, and HM Inspector's going to have his hand out to you.'

'Oh, not now, Maurice,' Jennie groaned. 'I've only just woken up.'

'Has to be considered,' he said with loathsome cheerfulness. 'You're having lunch with me today, by the way. We've a lot to discuss. Apart from anything else, the news that you were grabbed at your first evening by Mick West will have a salutary effect on the opposition. Don't forget we've got to negotiate the new *Eagle* contract. If I can go in there armed to the teeth with rival offers—'

'You do love playing games, don't you,' Jennie said, smiling. 'You and the other big kids. I know, Maurice, and you know, that they'll pay exactly what they expect to pay, and exactly what I expect them to pay, but you'll have an awful lot of fun first looking narrow-eyed and dangerous at each other.'

'Never try to strip a man of his illusions, Jennie,' Maurice said seriously. 'It leaves him with nothing to lose.'

'I know all about having nothing to lose,' she said. 'You go ahead and play, Maurice. That's what I pay you for.'

She imagined him wincing. 'Mentioning money at a time like this,' he said, sucking his teeth. 'You're too crude for me. Women are always more atavistic than men. Earthy. No poetry. I thought our relationship meant more to you than simply one of employer-employee.'

'I thought our relationship meant more to you than foisting me off on Quin when I was in need of moral support.'

This time his voice implied spread hands. 'He told me you were old friends. So I took him at his word? So I made a mistake. Sue me.'

'I never thought to hear you say that word, darling. Where are we meeting for lunch?'

'Come to the office and we'll decide there.'

'And find myself met by the second eleven again. No thanks. You call for me here.'

'She has no faith. All right. I'll pick you up at twelve-fifteen.'

Jennie put down the telephone, and remembered Miss Brodie. 'He thinks to intimidate me with the use of the quarter-hour,' she muttered. She stretched and yawned. 'Bath,' she said aloud, brightening, and then, 'Real breakfast.' She smiled and jumped out of bed.

Maurice was on time, which she appreciated. He had changed so little in the intervening five years that she thought he was still wearing the same suit. It had been made to last, however, so that was not necessarily a criticism. He kissed her on both cheeks.

'You look wonderful,' he said.

'You never used to kiss me hullo, Maurice,' she said. 'I must be more famous than I thought.'

'Always after the third book published,' he explained. 'I shake hands for two books, the third book I kiss one cheek—'

'Don't go on. I dread to think what will happen when I reach twenty. And, thank you very much, but I don't look wonderful. All my clothes are five years old and ten years unfashionable. That's why I left most of them behind. I'm going to sublimate my grief by shopping.'

'That's what I meant. For a woman in your position, you look wonderful. You'd never know if you didn't know. How are you, really?' His voice changed abruptly from banter to seriousness. She shrugged.

'I'll survive,' she said. There was something about Maurice's briskness that made her speak with almost Yiddish elipsis.

'I know *that*,' he said. 'That wasn't the question. Is the hotel all right? Mary says to tell you you can stay with us if you'd prefer.'

'That's very kind, but I'd sooner be on my own for the time being. Tell her thank you all the same, but no.'

Now he shrugged. 'I already did,' he said. They walked down to St Martin's Lane to a little French restaurant, fashionably obscure and good without being pretentious.

Jennie discovered she was hungry, which after the breakfast she had consumed only two and a half hours ago was downright unhealthy. She chose *crêpes* stuffed with prawns and rice and onions and mushrooms to start with, and steak *tartare* to follow.

'Oh, beef,' she cried ecstatically. 'After five years of lamb and kid, lamb and kid. And if I see another salad, I shall turn into a greenfly.'

'You used to write you loved the food,' Maurice accused.

'I do. I like variety, that's all. And oh God, French wines! Quin gave me real burgundy last night. I thought I'd died and gone to heaven.'

'You choose the wine today,' Maurice suggested generously.

'A claret,' she said promptly. 'I know with steak *tartare* and all that—but I can't help it. I must have a claret.'

Maurice shrugged. 'I'm no wine-snob. A claret you want, a claret you shall have. There's a Mouton Cadet here, 1973. That do you?'

Jennie groaned expressively, and turned her eyes resolutely away from the prices. Time enough to find how *that* side of things had gone. For one day more she would allow herself to revel and be treated. The *crêpes* came, and Maurice's melon, and he began to talk.

'Now then. You can forget what Mick West said last night about a promo tour. You'll be going with Firmans. It's to be next month, when the new *Eagle* comes out, and they've already got quite excited about it.'

'Isn't this a bit of a volte-face? It was your idea to let Quin take me out.'

'Never mind. That was all a bit of PR work. Mandersons never did a promo in their lives. He knows that and I know that. What he's after is the new contract. Besides, how can you do a personal tour when you aren't who you're supposed to be, tell me that? A pseudonym signing books and going on the telly? Nonsense.'

'Oh,' Jennie said, humbled.

'Firmans will do it right—they don't mess around. Their

organisation is good and they're prepared to go all out with this. And that way you'll get your name before the public and the trade just in time for me to negotiate with Cavelle.'

'Wait a minute, you're going too fast for me. What's this about Cavelle?'

'Cavelle have approached me about a new series they want to do. They've asked me if I can recommend anyone to write it—so of course I recommended you.'

'Very kind of you—what sort of series?'

'Oh, your usual thing of course. But they've already said they'd want your name, and all this publicity will make it worth that much more.'

'But wait a minute, won't Firmans have something to say about that?'

'They can *say* what they like. They only have the options on the next *Eagle* book. Cavelles want Gothic romances with plenty of sex and mystery, frissons and frolic. Quite different. Firmans can't touch it. And if they want you to go exclusive, they'll have to pay, won't they?'

'Oh Maurice, you are a devious bugger,' Jennie said admiringly. He lifted his hands.

'Please. You know I don't like ladies to swear. And everything I do, I do as it ought to be done. Please don't suggest I'm anything except a hundred per cent.'

'Don't tell me you're putting your commission up!'

Even *he* laughed at that. He stepped out of his persona for a moment and said, 'Actually, I think they've already heard about it.'

'On Ye Olde Magic Grapevine, presumably,' Jennie murmured. He nodded.

'Anyway, I think they've heard enough to get nervous, because this morning I had a telephone call from Angus Mitchell himself—and he didn't reverse the charges!'

Jennie knew enough to know this was just about a joke. 'What did he want?'

'He wanted to know if it would be a good idea to invite you to dinner at his house this evening. You've never met, I believe.'

'No. He took over after I'd left the country.'

'He said he thought you might be at a loss, alone in the town, no friends perhaps, living in a hotel room. Would it be a kind thing to ask you to his house for dinner and to stay the night.'

'That *is* kind,' Jennie said, touched. Maurice cocked his head like a knowing bird.

'Don't suppose it. He knows the value of a gesture. But I said you'd go, anyway. You should meet him, and better you should meet him on those terms. But don't talk business. If he tries to bring it up, steer him away, change the subject, or just act dumb. Keep it social, and you'll be all right. He'll be at a disadvantage because you'll know what he's up to, but he won't know you know.'

Jennie shook her head.

'I can't keep up with all this. Can't I just go as myself, and take people as I find them?'

'You're too old to be that young,' Maurice said. 'Naïvety like that is sheer sophistication.' He regarded her with his head slightly to one side. 'However,' he went on speculatively, 'on you it might just work. Could be fetching. Try it if you like, but be careful.'

Jennie started to laugh. 'Maurice, I meant it literally,' she protested. His face straightened, and his eyes smiled.

'I know. I tease you. Come, empty your glass. If I drink my half of this I shall be incapable all afternoon, and I have business to do. I might be nice to someone, think of that!' he pronounced in tones of horror. Jennie caught the hand he was stretching across the table for her glass, and raised it to her lips.

'Maurice, I do love you,' she said, kissing it. 'And after lunch I shall have to go shopping for a new dress to be beguiling in, so I'd better not get too plastered either. I don't want to end up with any old schmutter, do I?'

'The words you come out with!' he said with cockney horror, and she began to laugh. It occurred to her she hadn't laughed like that for a very long time.

CHAPTER SEVEN

SHOPPING THAT afternoon was a revelation to Jennie. She spent far more than she had anticipated, but on the other hand she liked what she bought far more than she had expected to. The shop girl to whom she explained her circumstances said, 'You're lucky you came back this year. Last year the clothes were dreadful, really ugly. The colours this year are nice.'

With the example of Bea before her, Jennie knew what she wanted—clothes that were both pretty and outrageous. She would change her image, get back the five years she had lost, spent mouldering in the backest of backwaters; she intended to do what she wanted from now on, and to have fun. She was aware, of course, that some of this resolve stemmed from bitterness, but what the hell? It didn't make it any less exciting to contemplate that if Bea was all anxiousness to change places with her, the least she could expect of life was that she should change places with Bea. Who knows, maybe she would have the best of the bargain.

If Angus Mitchell's invitation was pure professionalism, at least it was carried right through in a professional manner: when she returned from her shopping expedition to her hotel there was a message at the desk informing her that a car would collect her and take her to the Mitchell house. She was grateful for the thoughtfulness. It had not yet occurred to her, but when she read the message she realised that in an hour at the latest she would have been worrying about how to get there.

She had a bath and washed her hair, and then did her make-up and dressed. She chose a pair of white silk harem pants and a pink lurex boobtube of a shade that made the most of her Cretan sun-tan, and of a brevity that revealed a good deal of her midriff as well as her shoulders and back. Into her overnight bag she packed her washing things and a cotton nightdress in case she had to go to the loo in the night—she never wore anything in bed—and a pretty poly-cotton dress for the next day. There was nothing more sordid, in her view, than putting on the party clothes of the night before when you haven't slept in your own bed. As a last thought she put in her bedtime reading of the moment—an Evelyn Waugh—in case she should find herself unable to sleep. She had a horror of being stranded anywhere without a book.

The Mitchells' house, the driver told her, was in Bedford Park, which sounded remote and High Wycombish to Jennie, but turned out to be very nearly the same thing as Chiswick. The driver spoke so knowledgeably about the place that Jennie was constrained to ask if he was a friend of the family, and thereby discovered that Firmans had an account with the minicab firm in question and that her driver often drove Angus Mitchell home after late board meetings. The information allayed another doubt she had begun to have, as to whether or not she would be expected to pay the driver.

The house was large and beautiful and Edwardian, and stood in a secluded street of equally large and beautiful Edwardian houses which managed to be just like it and yet quite different. Jennie half expected the door to be opened by a servant, and indeed would have found that to be less unnerving than what actually happened; the door was opened to her by a man of such startling beauty that for a moment she could do nothing but stare at him.

'Hullo, Jennie! I'm Angus. Do come in,' he said. 'I only

just recognise you from your photographs. I see now that we shall have to get some new ones for our files—the ones we have don't do you any justice at all.'

'Hullo,' Jennie said, belatedly. Angus Mitchell was tall, well-built in a lithe sort of way like an athlete, and stunningly handsome. His hair was thick and glossy and very dark, almost black, his skin very pale as sometimes Scots are, his eyes vividly blue above the kind of pushed-up cheekbones that Rudolf Nureyev made fashionable. His features were classically, Byronically handsome, his hands long and slim, and his casual clothes breathed wealth and privilege—pale grey slacks of a fine woollen facecloth, a cashmere jumper of the only shade of blue that would do anything for his eyes, soft leather moccasins that were probably hand-made.

Angus was shaking her hand and looking her over in the interested, unchallenging way that one good-looking person always examines another—a kind of freemasonry of attractiveness.

'I'm so glad you could come,' he went on. 'Just dump your little bag in the hall. Do you want to go upstairs first? Fine, then come on in and have a drink. It's really wonderful to meet you at last, although I'm sorry for your sake it had to be in these particular circumstances.'

'It was kind of you to think of asking me,' Jennie said. Such was Angus's warmth that she already felt it *had* been kindness, and not professionalism.

'Not at all,' he demurred politely. He had no Scottish accent at all; in fact his diction was so exquisite you might have been forgiven for thinking English was not his native language. 'It must be lonely for you, coming back after so long. I guessed you might be at a loss just at first. Now, do come into the drawing room and meet my wife.'

He pushed open a door and ushered her into the kind of long, high-ceilinged room that inevitably had stained-and-polished bare floorboards and an extremely valuable Persian rug in the centre. Jennie took in the Adam fireplace, the enormous leather chesterfield, the discreetly antique furniture, the dark velvet curtains, and the rather gloomy oil paintings on the walls, before her attention was called to the only other occupant of the room.

'Jennie, my wife, Daisy. Darling, Jennie Savage.'

They shook hands. Daisy murmured, 'Delighted to meet you,' and Jennie found herself saying, 'How do you do?' like a teenager who has been taught etiquette. On consideration, Daisy was the only kind of woman who could have coped with Angus's beauty. She was one of those tall, large-boned, fair-skinned English beauties whose superior size speaks of years of careful breeding and healthy food. She had a pale, sculpted face whose purity of line made her look more like an alabaster statue of a Greek god than a human woman, and a mane of hair of that beautiful red-gold colour that nothing out of a bottle can ever reproduce. If Angus breathed out wealth and privilege, she breathed wealth, privilege and aristocracy. Jennie felt herself dwindling. Any more of this, she thought, and I'll end up as a small stain on the carpet.

'What will you have to drink?' Angus was asking her.

'What's good for shock?' she said aloud. 'A whisky, I think.'

'Anything in it?'

'No, just as it comes. Straight from the cow,' she said.

'A woman after my own heart,' Angus said. 'I can't bear to see the way you English adulterate good Scotch with water and ice and sodapops.'

'You English indeed,' Daisy said. Her voice was so beautifully modulated that Jennie found it hard to hear what she said, being occupied in listening to the sound of it. 'You'd never think to hear Angus that he was born in London, went through Eton, Oxford and the Guards, and never set foot in Scotland until he was twenty-three. And whisky doesn't come from cows. And why are you shocked?'

'Here's your drink,' Angus said, handing her the sort of heavy-bottom tumbler she had always wanted to own and saving her from having to answer Daisy's question. 'Are you all right, darling? Do you want a refill?'

'Yes please,' Daisy said, handing over her glass. The

marble profile came round towards Jennie. 'Why are you shocked?' she asked again. Jennie had misjudged her.

'Everything is so different,' she said.

'Different from what?'

From what she had expected, of course, but she was not prepared to say that. She had not expected such wealth, such elegance, such beauty, and if she had expected it, she would not have expected to feel so much at home in it, but all she said was 'From Crete.'

'I suppose it would be,' Daisy said, losing interest. Angus caught Jennie's eye and she saw that he knew she had not answered the question.

'You're different too,' he said with a wicked glint in his eyes. 'Of course, we'd seen your photo on the file, but there was no knowing how long ago that was taken, or your resemblance to it. Knowing you were a romantic novelist, we thought you'd be around fifty, with a terrifying perm.'

'And rows of those coloured glass beads round your neck,' Daisy added.

'And probably a bright green tweed suit with a mix'n'match twinset—'

'And maybe even a silk scarf—'

'Patterned, of course,' Angus finished, grinning triumphantly.

'Is that what romantic novelists are like?' Jennie asked, intrigued.

'Inevitably,' Daisy said.

'Invariably,' Angus added.

'What you probably failed to take into account,' Jennie said seriously, 'is that I'm not a romantic novelist.'

'Oh? What are you, then?' Angus asked.

'A professional. A hack. A work-horse. I write for other publishers too, you know.'

He frowned and came towards her menacingly. 'You're not allowed to say that sort of thing here. It offends my sensibilities. And, whatever you do,' he lowered his voice to a stage whisper, 'don't mention the names in front of my wife. She's delicate.' Daisy performed a creditable half-swoon.

'Have another drink,' Angus finished abruptly. Jennie yielded up her glass. They were turning out to be much less daunting than she had expected.

'You aren't a bit like a publisher, I may as well tell you,' she said as Angus went back to the drinks table. 'You ought to be either over seventy, six-foot-five tall and gaunt, or else around sixty and portly, with a nose that speaks of expense-account lunches and a silk cravat. And really, the pair of you are quite indecently handsome. You've no right—no right at all.'

They were both laughing now. Daisy said, 'If you think Angus is handsome, you ought to see his son by his first marriage. That boy ought to be locked up—I've said so time and time again. He's a hazard to female motorists.'

'You're exaggerating a teeny weeny bit, aren't you, darling?' Angus said, looking pleased.

'Not very much. This is true, Jennie; I was walking along the road with him one day and a woman passed driving a car and she was within a hairsbreadth of driving into a tree because she couldn't take her eyes off Jason.'

'You called him Jason?' Jennie said to Angus as she took her drink. He shrugged.

'I had to give the little blighter some disadvantage to counteract his looks and his intelligence. So I called him Jason and divorced his mother.'

'Darling, I don't think we ought to mention that subject tonight,' Daisy said. 'Jennie won't want to be reminded.'

'I don't see how we can avoid it, in the circumstances,' Angus replied and then turned to Jennie. 'The only other guest tonight is my brother Nick, and he's staying here because he's just got divorced and hasn't anywhere to live. So with you and him and the memory of me—it would be like dining with Cyrano de Bergerac and trying not to mention the word nose.'

Daisy looked at her watch. 'Where is Nick, anyway? If he doesn't come soon, my dinner will be spoiled, and you know I love to show off my accomplishments.'

'I'll go and rout him out,' Angus said, and explained to

Jennie, 'He was late home from work, and he was still in the bath when you arrived, but he ought to be finished now. He's a barrister. I sometimes wonder if all this compulsive washing when he gets home is a touch of the Pontius Pilate syndrome. I notice it's always worse when he's been in court.'

Daisy watched Angus leave the room her love for him in her eyes. Turning to Jennie, she said, 'Poor Nick's had a bad time, actually. He was crazy about Diana, and then she ran off with a man half his age, and that must have done terrible things to his ego. He was awfully noble about it, and let her divorce him. He just lives for his work now. Angus, of course, loves him terribly, and worries over him even more than he worries over Jason.'

'It's nice to find brothers loving each other,' Jennie said. 'Which is the elder?'

'Nick is, by five years. They're only half-brothers, actually. They weren't brought up together. They first met when Angus was twelve, just the right age to hero-worship Nick, and when Angus's parents split up, Nick took care of Angus, so the impression never dimmed.' She paused and looked at Jennie consideringly. 'I don't know whether I ought to say this,' she began slowly, 'but I think perhaps I ought to warn you about Nick—' She broke off abruptly, for there was the sound of voices and footsteps outside. 'Here they are,' she muttered, and said no more. Jennie was left to wonder what she had been about to be warned of, but the door opened, and Angus came in, closely followed by his brother.

Jennie's first thought was that everything about Nick, while wildly, absurdly like Angus, differed in just that slight degree that made the difference between good looks and plainness. Nick was a fraction taller and a fraction thinner, and he stooped slightly. His face was a little longer; his nose just too big and sharp, his chin just too long, his mouth just too thin. In any drawing room, all eyes would be drawn to Angus's astounding beauty, and Nick would pass unnoticed.

'Here we are at last. Jennie, may I introduce my big

brother Nicholas? Nick, this is our star author, Jennie Savage.'

Nick came forward and held out his hand; Jennie took it, and looked up into his face.

'How do you do,' Nick said. It would be an exaggeration to say that Jennie actually heard cannon fire, fireworks and bells, or saw water playing in floodlit fountains, but she stared at Nick as though she had just been hit over the head with a rubber mallet. For much of her life she had written about just such encounters as these with all the confidence of one who knows they do not actually happen in real life. She looked up into Nick's eyes—they were *gold*, one part of her mind commented in surprise, gold and slanting like a Cretan's, not blue like Angus's—and felt her insides turning to water. Her feelings on encountering Angus's fabled looks had been of amused interest, but Nick, lacking in every dimension that perfect beauty, made her feel weak and dizzy. He was looking at her with much the same expression she thought must be on her face. That she did not instantly rip off all his clothes was a feat of self-restraint comparable to owning a Scottie dog and not buying it a tartan collar.

'My God,' was what she actually said. Nick gave a crooked smile that turned up more one side than the other.

'I know what you mean,' he croaked. The exchange was too low for the other couple to have heard, but the way they were staring at each other, and holding hands as if they'd just signed a suicide pact was obvious enough. Daisy felt constrained at least to intervene.

'Would you like a drink, Nick? Dinner will be five minutes, now that you're here.'

There was a hint of reproach in the last few words which he acknowledged only by a flicker of amusement in the golden eyes which otherwise steadily held Jennie's gaze. Angus now made hasty amends.

'You go ahead with the dinner, darling. I'll get Nick a drink.' Daisy left the room with a shrug as Angus went across to the drinks table.

'You have the most beautiful hair I've ever seen in my life,'

Nick said quietly. 'But there isn't enough of it. You must grow it.'

'I will,' Jennie said. Angus came across with a tumbler and looked at them with amusement.

'Here you are, Nick. If you could possibly give her back her hand and take this—'

Nick released Jennie's hand, and she looked down at her fingers, amazed to discover they had not been charred like barbecued chipolatas.

'Would you like another?' Angus asked her. 'I think you need it.'

'Thanks,' she said.

'And by the way, pay no attention to Nick. He isn't half as good looking or half as intelligent as me. He's a barrister, and you know what that means.'

'He's maligning me for his own ends,' Nick said. His voice was as beautiful as Angus's, but without that slightly foreign-sounding formality. 'He wants to keep you to himself.'

'What does it mean to be a barrister?' Jennie asked.

'He's implying I'm a cold fish,' Nick said. 'But I'm sure you know better, don't you?'

'How should she know better?' Angus asked, coming back with Jennie's drink. She gulped at it by mistake, and coughed.

'She's just looked right through to the back of my skull,' Nick answered.

'Ah, yes, she did that to me, too. Why do you look at people like that, you disconcerting young woman?'

'I suppose,' Jennie said, 'that it's a habit I got into in Crete. The Cretans always look straight at you when they talk. It would be considered rude not to. And neither of you was the least disconcerted.'

Angus made a face. 'I forgot, we're dealing with a writer here. They notice things. You have been warned, Nick.'

'You live in Crete?' Nick asked. Was there a hint of disappointment in his voice?

'Up until two days ago,' Jennie replied.

'It would have been more romantic to say up until two minutes ago,' Nick demurred.

'But not honest,' Jennie said. 'And I will never tell you anything but the truth.'

'She's left her husband,' Angus explained.

'I'm getting divorced,' Jennie added. 'He prefers a friend of mine.'

'Madman,' Nick commented dispassionately.

'That's what I thought. Still, his loss is our gain, and all that sort of thing. How much of this can you take, Jennie?' Angus enquired.

'As much as you like to hand out,' Jennie said, laughing with a sudden feeling of lightheadedness. Could her second drink have gone to her head? 'My appetite for flattery is insatiable.'

Angus sighed. 'Another bloody author. It's lucky I have a natural talent for creeping. I think we'd better go into the dining room and sit down. Make a good impression. Jennie, will you allow me?' He offered his arm in a superfluously courteous gesture, and Nick struck it away.

'Hands off,' he said. Angus shrugged, smiled, and walked ahead of them out of the room. Nick smiled down for a moment longer at Jennie and said, surprisingly, 'It's all right, you know.'

The observant, note-taking, writer's part of her brain jotted this down and wondered what, if anything, it meant; but another part, which she had not suspected herself of owning, knew exactly what he was talking about, and she heard herself saying yes, as if consenting to a proposition. Then there didn't seem to be anything else to do but follow Angus, and feel Nick coming along behind her as if like a salamander he could endure the flames while she was merely a paper cut-out.

It was a wonderful dinner. Daisy had prepared the kind of dishes one normally expects to get only in the more expensive restaurants, and Jennie apologised silently for having been about to suspect her of fussing unduly over the dinner being spoilt. When one goes to the trouble Daisy had evidently gone to, one has a right to expect one's guests to be an audience as well. The wine, still a novelty to Jennie after five years of retsina and domestica, was good enough to make her feel privileged without being so good as to make her feel guilty.

Nick talked about the court case he was conducting at that moment.

'I think tomorrow could be the last day,' he said.

'And will you get him off?' Angus asked.

'Not a doubt of it,' Nick said. 'Provided I can keep him out of the witness box. He has all a criminal's natural love of performance.'

'I don't think you ought to call him a criminal,' Daisy said. 'After all, a man is innocent until proved guilty.' Nick shrugged in a way that Jennie felt she could interpret without difficulty.

'You think he's guilty?'

'I do.'

'But you still defend him?'

'It's my job,' he said.

'Your job to defend people without believing in their innocence?'

'And is it your job to write books without believing in the sentiments expressed in them?' Nick asked her. She accepted the justice of the remark.

'But that must make us awfully shifty characters, mustn't it?'

'All writers are shifty,' Angus said. 'You lived with one for however many years. You ought to know that. You never know what a writer's thinking. They're smiling at you and nodding and agreeing, and underneath it all, making mental notes with which later on they'll destroy you in a thinly disguised satire.'

Jennie glanced round at Angus in surprise, and saw to her relief that he was himself satirising.

'Darling, you mustn't generalise,' Daisy reproved gently.

'All generalisations are false,' Nick said.

It took Jennie a moment or two to catch up with that one. Meanwhile she was saying to Angus, 'How do you know that

that is the most common accusation levelled at a writer?'

He laughed. 'My dear girl, I've been working with them all my adult life. And if there's one thing you can be sure of discussing with authors, it's themselves.'

'Oh, well,' Jennie said ruefully, 'in that case I'll shut up.' She was intensely aware that Nick's ankle was being rubbed slowly and caressingly up and down her calf. 'Instead, tell me about the tour.'

'What's to tell? You'll love it.'

'You will not,' Daisy interrupted. 'They're absolute hell, Jennie, but very good for trade. You'll be on the road for hours of every day, and they'll be the only times you sit down. To make it worth while you have to really bustle, and after the first few mad dashes through town centre traffic, you'll begin to think you've gone mad.'

'That's constructive,' Angus said witheringly. 'And what will you do when she decides not to do it after all?'

'Oh, she won't,' Daisy said easily. 'She has too much sense of duty for that. You never were a very good judge of character, Angus.'

'Yes, but remember she's in a highly emotional state.'

'All the more reason why she'll plunge herself into work, to forget. Trust me—I have an insight into feminine psychology.'

'Where did you get it from?' Angus said with interest. 'If they've got any left I could do with a couple.'

Jennie watched the conversation being batted back and forth like someone at a tennis match. She looked at Nick—she only needed an excuse.

'Are they always like this?'

'Invariably. Shall we leave them to it? We could go upstairs to my room and have a look at my French engravings.'

'Might that not be a bit rude?'

'Exactly what I was hoping.' Nick gave her a mock leer, and Jennie slipped her foot out of her shoe and slid it up his trouser leg, and was rewarded by the sight of his unprepared start.

'I prefer etchings myself,' she said.

'I've got some etchings in my room,' Angus said eagerly. Daisy put a kind and restraining hand on his arm.

'No, darling, they're posters of Brigitte Bardot. Etchings are something quite different.'

'Curse. Foiled again.' Angus bared his teeth. Daisy smiled across at Jennie.

'Shall we leave them to it, these two idiots? I'll show you your room, if you'll come with me, and then you'll be able to go up whenever you feel you've had enough.'

Outside she looked at Jennie with a kind and curious look. 'Are you all right? They aren't too much for you, are they? They get a bit drunk on words, I think. I'm used to them, but if you're feeling a bit flattened, don't hesitate to speak up.'

'No, I'm enjoying it,' Jennie said.

'Are you? Good. Well, look, here's your room, and there's the bathroom, and you just go to bed as early or as late as you like. If you want to be on your own we'll understand. It must have been a hard couple of days for you.'

'Thanks. I'm all right, though, really. I'm enjoying the company.'

Daisy hesitated as if she were about to say something serious, and then she obviously changed her mind and began to lead the way downstairs again.

'That's our room, by the way, in case you should need anything in the night,' she said, pointing out the door. Jennie tried and failed to imagine herself knocking at it to ask for a glass of water at four o'clock in the morning.

'Thanks,' she said, feeling that covered the case. She would have liked to ask which room was Nick's—just out of interest—but it would not have done.

CHAPTER EIGHT

IT WAS about one o'clock when they all trooped up to bed, and Jennie had drunk herself into a state of euphoria. She cleaned her teeth, washed her face, and went to her bedroom, where she quickly took off her clothes, piling them neatly on a chair, and placed her cotton wrap handy to the bedside against midnight trips to the loo. There was no bedside lamp, which was awkward, so she drew back the curtains, thinking the light outside would suffice for reaching the bed from the light switch over by the door. However, when she turned off the light, it was pitch dark in the room. The window looked out on the garden and the neighbouring gardens, and there was no light. Feeling her way to the bed, she barked her skins painfully on the chair that held her clothes.

The bed, once she was in it, was blissfully comfortable, and she would have drifted off to sleep instantly had she not drunk so much that she was wakeful. She folded her arms comfortably under her head and looked through the darkness towards the window illuminated by just the faintest glimmer of light. It was blissfully quiet after Bloomsbury and her thoughts expanded in the silence.

She had not really—had she?—felt what she remembered feeling when she met Nick. It was not possible. And yet when he had looked down at her she had felt, or at least now remembered feeling, that here at last was the one person she had been meant to meet right from the beginning. Miles had been a diversion, a bit of irrelevant re-routing, and now she was back on the right road. But it was ridiculous. There was no such thing as love at first sight, as she, who made a reasonable living out of it, know better than anyone else. She could not have fallen instantly in love with Nick Mitchell. She must have imagined the whole thing.

She drifted to sleep, awakening with a start that made her whole body instantly rigid. She could actually feel the hairs rising on her head, at the slight sound that had jerked her into complete wakefulness. The door opened quietly, and a tall figure crossed quickly from the door to the bed—she saw the faint outline as it passed through the light from the window. It all happened too quickly for her to feel more than the first stirrings of fear, and then hands were feeling along the outside of the bed, and she felt the mattress dip under her as the bedclothes were pulled away and a weight came down.

'Move over,' a voice whispered. Her skin prickling all over with surprise and excitement and longing, she moved sideways, as he slipped in under the covers. She gasped—he was naked, and the touch of his silky warm skin against hers was like electricity. He wasted no time in talk, but wriggled down into the bed and drew her against him, wrapping his arms and legs around her and folding her lovingly against his chest. She had no doubts about the propriety of the act: she was in love, as he was, and there was nothing to keep them apart. Her arms went up round his neck, and as her breasts were crushed against his chest, he sighed, a sigh of enormous, quivering content.

There seemed no hurry. They were both content to rest like that for a while, cheek to cheek and no part of their bodies but that was touching. Then, very slowly, he slid his mouth round to hers. For a moment his warm, silky lips rested on hers enquiringly, and she breathed in the scent of him, knowing in advance how he would taste. Then his tongue came forward, hard and pointed, to part her lips and teeth and work deep into her mouth. She gulped, tasting him, drinking his saliva in a sudden ecstasy of abandonment. She felt her whole body become loose and soft, as if she were disintegrating, and she clung, weakly, wanting him with an enormous and helpless passion as if she were consumed with a fever.

All her senses were swollen with it—taste and touch and smell and sound. Her nerve-endings hurt as if his skin was red-hot, the sound of his breathing hurt her ears, her face felt huge and ultra-sensitive like one enormous bruise. His hands began to move about her body, stroking and touching and caressing her into agony. She felt him grow hard against her groin, but she was so helpless with love she could do nothing about it. His mouth left hers and kissed her eyes and cheeks, and then her neck, and then he bent his head to her breast and her hands moved weakly to stroke his hair, feeling the hard, satisfying shape of his skull under her fingers. He kissed her nipple taking it in his mouth, rolling it between his tongue and teeth until it was hard, and then closing his mouth over it, he sucked.

She had never known a man who knew how to do that. Miles had always been too gentle, and she had hardly felt it, and had had to pretend a pleasure. She felt her womb contract at the insistent tug, felt herself melting again with impossible bliss, and she held his head in her two hands as if he were a child and longed to give him milk from her breast, longed actually to feed him. His hands were moving down her flanks now, and he was moving his weight across her, settling it centrally. He released her nipple, to her piercing loss, instantly assuaged as he clamped his mouth over the other breast.

His fingers ran over her belly and thighs, sliding downwards over the inner curves, and she parted before them like the Red Sea before Moses. Her whole body seemed to open outwards like a flower, and as she felt him change his weight again she knew an anticipation of pleasure that was as piercing as pain. She felt that she would quite literally die if he did not come into her then, and her hands pressed at his back, urging him towards her. Then that touch, so different from the touch of any other skin, and she cried out in an agony of sensation as he slid readily into her. As he moved gently, he placed a tender hand across her mouth to remind her that they were not alone in the house, and she was glad of it, for she was beyond controlling herself now. She fastened her teeth in his palm, and as he moved once more she came violently in a series of explosions that jerked her body against him as if she were in the throes of an epileptic fit.

He held her, containing her movements with his stillness, and with a sensitivity she had scarcely expected he was careful not to move again until her convulsions had stopped. Then, very carefully, he removed his hand from her mouth and kissed her lips tenderly. His lips were salty, and when she placed her own against his cheek, it was wet, though whether with tears or sweat she did not know. She felt dazed, unutterably vulnerable, as if what had happened to her had snapped something inside her, something that held her self to her body—her soul or mind or whatever it was that was the essence of her. If he had done the wrong thing then, her self might have been lost for ever. But he held her until she stopped shaking before he began to move again.

Long ripples of pleasure ran through her, growing at each thrust, and each slow withdrawal. His hands were still now, his sensations she knew were concentrated on that one pin-point of pleasure, and his breathing grew laboured, as if he were running uphill. She moved with him, no longer helpless, lifting to meet each forward surge like a boat lifting its bow to the sea. Then the whole tone of his skin changed, and she felt him gather inside her like a cat preparing to spring, and she held him tighter, protectively, as with a muffled cry he came too, emptying himself into her like a libation.

For a long time they were silent, lying collapsed against each other, spent as dead matches, and Jennie drifted away and back, spinning slowly out into the darkness with a sense of absolute disintegration, only to be drawn back to the reality of the warm weight of him on top of her and the lovingness of his cheek against her own. He slept. She knew by the feel of his skin and the sound of his breathing that he had fallen instantly asleep, just as she knew when he woke again. At last he turned his head and kissed her cheek.

'Is this really happening?' she asked in a whisper.

'I think so,' he whispered back. 'You knew, didn't you, from the moment we met?'

'Yes,' she said. They were silent again, and then he shifted his weight from her to lie beside her, placing her head on to his shoulder, then folding his arms around her. She snuggled in, happily. It was her favourite of all positions, the one in which she felt safest, happiest, most loved.

'Are you comfortable?' he asked.

'Yes,' she said, and it seemed inadequate to express all she was feeling. *I'm too happy to be asleep*, she thought. *It would be a waste.* And almost instantly on that thought, she fell asleep.

When she woke it was growing light, and she was alone. She was so sure that he could not have got out of bed without her noticing, that she thought it must all have been a dream, and in deep disappointment she turned on to her side and fell asleep again. When she woke next, and more fully, she knew it had happened. The sensations of her body, the wetness, the smell of sweat and semen all told her that it had really happened. She looked at her watch. It was half past eight. Why had he gone so early? Why had he not finished the night in her bed?

She knew what she had felt, but the habit of self-doubt was not so easy to shake off, and already she was beginning to wonder about his motives. It wasn't likely, was it, that he had felt what she had felt? It wasn't likely to have been love—more likely simply lust. Restless, she got up and went for a bath, wanting to linger and soak but unable to relax even to that extent. While she was dressing afterwards in her room she heard the sound of movement downstairs, and she hurried, fumbling with zips and buttons, so that she would be able to stroll down casually and confront him in the kitchen. She dashed for the door, remembered she hadn't done her hair and went back to do it, and then strolled casually down the stairs and into the kitchen, where Daisy, alone, was making tea.

'Oh, you're up! I was going to bring you up a cup of tea in bed,' she said, smiling.

'That would have been nice,' Jennie said, controlling her disappointment. 'For two pins I'd go back and get in again.'

'How did you sleep?'

'Very well, thanks. I didn't even dream,' Jennie said. Does she really not know? or at least guess?

'I did too, but Angus was restless. He kept getting up. Too much booze, I expect. He's out getting the paper. The boy is supposed to deliver, but he doesn't get here until ten most mornings, and that's too late to be any good. It's no use telling them, though. Nick has gone to work, of course.

'Of course,' Jennie echoed. A pang of disappointment. She would not even have the pleasure of breakfasting with him. She would not have the very necessary reassurance of seeing his face, reading his feelings in his eyes.

'He goes early most days to miss the traffic, but he was extra early today, I suppose because of his court case. I heard him go out. How do you like your tea?'

'Strong, please,' she said. Daisy poured a cup and handed it to her, and continued to look at her steadily so that Jennie was forced at last to shake off her dejection and raise an enquiring eyebrow.

'Jennie,' Daisy began hesitatingly. 'Look, it isn't any of my business, but—well, I couldn't help noticing last night—or at least I thought I did—that you seemed a bit—well—struck with Nicholas.'

'He's a very attractive man,' Jennie said non-committally.

'M'yes, I know—that's the trouble. I remember when I first met him, and he bowed over my hand as if I were Helen of Troy. He's so charming, he has a way of making you feel special.'

'I gather,' Jennie said, sipping her tea as an excuse not to meet Daisy's lovely eyes, 'that what you're trying to tell me is that he behaves that way to everyone, and that I shouldn't take any notice of it.'

'Well, it would be hard not to take any notice of it,' Daisy said with unexpected humanity. 'But if you wouldn't take a warning amiss, I'd hint that perhaps you shouldn't take it too seriously.' Jennie looked at her then, and wondered whether Daisy had any idea that he had visited her bedroom last night. Daisy's expression was unfathomable, and if she was longing to ask that very question, she was hiding it very well.

'Don't worry about me,' Jennie said bravely, 'I'm impervious to charm. Look how easily I resist Angus.'

It was meant as a joke, but Daisy was suddenly serious, and she turned to the window, sweeping her magnificent hair away from her face and looking out into the garden with unseeing eyes.

'Angus is easy,' she said. 'He's so beautiful there isn't room in him for anything else. He's as harmless and wholesome as milk. But Nick—he's like Milton's Satan. When I was first going out with Angus, and he kept talking about Nick and how wonderful he was—real hero-worship stuff—I got to hate the sound of his name. I sometimes think it was a forewarning. When I met Nick I fell in love with him instantly, at first sight, and I thought he had fallen in love with me. I didn't know what to do. I couldn't bear the idea of hurting Angus, but I loved Nick so much—' She paused, remembering. 'We had a wild affair for almost four months, and finally I said to Nick that we would have to tell Angus, that we couldn't go on deceiving him and Diana—he was still married then, of course. Instantly Nick cooled off. It was just a bit of fun for him. He didn't love me at all. We never went to bed again, and I married Angus, and you'd never know, even when we're alone together, that we'd ever been more than in-laws.'

There was a silence when she stopped, and after a moment Jennie said quietly, 'Thank you for telling me. It was brave of you.'

Daisy turned from the window. She looked even paler than before, and her eyes looked huge in her face. 'I wanted to warn you before you met him but there wasn't time. Then I saw you looking at him just the way I used to. He doesn't care for anyone but himself, any more than he cared for me. Oh, listen, I don't want you to think the wrong thing about me. I'm over him now—I love Angus. Angie is worth ten of Nick. I'm not being bitchy or anything—'

'I didn't think you were.'

'Thanks. Angus was worried last night too. He guessed about me and Nick. He's very intelligent, you know, and sensitive. Last night when we were getting undressed he said I ought to have locked your bedroom door. He said it in a jokey way, but I think I know what he meant. And then he couldn't sleep. He kept getting up and going out. I think he might have been checking that you hadn't been disturbed.'

How Jennie kept from blushing at that point she often wondered afterwards, but she felt that at least she had to settle the mind of her kind hostess.

'I'm all right,' she said. 'Really. I did think he was charming, but—' she let the implication hang, that it had been nothing more than that, and there was no need to explain further for at that moment Angus arrived with the papers.

'Ah, here's our prize authoress! Good morning. Have a good sleep?'

'Yes, thank you.'

'Good. That's more than I did. Too much rich food, I expect. I thought you might like a lift into town with me this morning. Actually, I had hoped you'd come to the office this morning to discuss the tour with our publicity people, but if you've got some other plans we can make another date. Only not too far into the future, because these things need time and if there are any little hitches—'

'I hadn't anything planned, other than that I have to phone Maurice at some time.'

'I know what that's for—to assure him that you haven't been corrupted and/or white-slaved by the wicked minions of Firman and Jackson. What agents never seem to realise is that we are actually on the same side.'

'They realise it,' Daisy put in. 'It's just that if they ever let their authors realise it, they'd be out of a job.'

'That's true,' Angus said. 'Hey, look at the time—it's nearly nine. Come on, Miss Savage, or should I say Ms Savage, now that you've entered the ranks of the unmarried—we must get weaving. Have you cleaned your teeth and said your prayers and all the appropriate things? Good. We'll be off, then. Bye, darling—I'll see you tonight.'

'Goodbye, Daisy, and thanks for a lovely evening,' Jennie said as Angus led the way towards the door. Daisy looked at her significantly for a moment, and then gave her a swift hug.

''Bye. Come again soon,' she said.

Angus seemed in great good humour, and hummed to himself as he drove away. He drove very fast and, as Jennie would have expected, competently, and concentrated on the turns until they were on the fast section of the A4. Then, he flicked a grin towards her and said, 'So you had a lovely evening, did you?'

'Yes, of course. Why should you doubt it?'

'I don't,' he said. 'But I wondered at one point whether you might be supposing you'd been cast in the role of a Christian to the family lion. But I see from your self-possession this morning that you withstood the attack very well.'

'I take it you are talking about Nick.'

'Of course, darling, who else? Naturally I wouldn't have subjected you to him unless I'd seen from the first moment you knew how to handle yourself. He does come on a bit strong sometimes, but it's purely habit with him. He doesn't mean anything by it.'

Jennie nodded glumly. All she needed now was to avoid it being discovered that she had made a fool of herself. So much for relying on instinct! She had been better off choosing a mate with reason, even if it had only turned out to be Miles. How could she have been such a fool? Because, she answered herself quickly, she wanted to be a fool—she wanted to believe, because of her bruised ego, that she had fallen in love and someone had fallen in love with her.

'I guessed that,' she said at last. 'People aren't often as charming as that without practising.'

'Oh, Nick gets a lot of practice. He's got at least three mistresses that I know of, and numerous less, shall we say, permanent girl-friends.'

'Daisy said he was mad about his wife,' Jennie could not help saying. Angus nodded.

'He was. I think that's part of the syndrome, proving to himself that he can do better than her. But I was afraid at one point last night that you might have a little visitor in your room. I expected from minute to minute to hear you screaming the roof down.'

Impossible this time not to go scarlet. Angus was fortunately busy watching the traffic behind him in order to pull out into the fast lane, and Jennie fixed her eyes on the road ahead while she regained her composure. Out of the corner of her eye she noticed that he was holding the steering-wheel rather oddly, with the tips of his fingers, and she glanced across just as he lifted his hand to scratch his eyebrow. There was a square pink elastoplast patch over the palm of his hand. His right hand. A bottomless pit opened up at her feet and she struggled hard not to fall down it.

Angus now turned to look at her, his face a mixture of amusement, curiosity and complicity plus several other things she did not even like to guess at. He turned his palm towards her and gave a little rueful shrug.

'Cut it on the lid of the tin when I was feeding the cat this morning. Funny place to get a cut, isn't it? I say, are you all right? You look a bit green. You're not going to be sick, are you? Shall I pull over somewhere?'

'No,' Jennie said with an effort. 'I'm all right. I won't be sick.'

'We'll be at the office in about fifteen minutes, but yell if you think you can't hold out until then.'

It had been dark, Jennie thought, and shied away from the memory of what she had imagined she felt. I think I'd rather like to die right now, this very instant.

* * *

The publicity person was a young man called Toby Chaplin who was the image of the young Paul McCartney with a Viva Zapata moustache and trousers so tightly fitting they left everything to be desired. He explained the itinerary to Jennie with an audience of Angus and a little blonde woman called Margie Smith who couldn't possibly be as young and gamine as she looked since she was the firm's head rep.

'The tour's for the series, of course, but since it's based on *The Eagle Flies* we'll be doing the first spot in Yorkshire, where the book's based. We'll do radio and a lunch in York itself and a quick tour of some bookshops, and then we'll go up to Richmond and get some pictures of you in Richmond Castle, and the Beeb have agreed to record you there for their local roundabout programme. We'll stay the night in Richmond and then on Tuesday we'll do Edinburgh, Wednesday, Glasgow, Thursday, Manchester, Friday, Bristol, and we'll get back to London for the grand finale on Saturday, press reception and trade dinner in the evening. Okay?'

'Gulp,' said Jennie. Toby grinned a white and engaging grin at her.

'Don't worry, Margie and I will be there to steer you through. You'll walk it. Any questions?'

'Just one—when do I get to wash my hair?'

Toby laughed, but Margie took it seriously. 'We'll be staying in first-class hotels. We can arrange for someone to come in and do it for you,' she said. Jennie smiled at the very idea.

'I'll manage,' she said, and then she remembered Nick saying how beautiful her hair was and she gulped again. Best not to think of things like that. She realised now, on mature consideration, that it was in the car she should have said something to Angus. By now it was much, much too late, and she could never now admit to him, whether it had been him or not, that she was not sure who it was who had visited her. That piece of folly would have to go unresolved; she would carry her ignorance to her grave, which would be punishment enough. Unless, of course, it had been Angus and he chose to enlighten her at some stage. She was not sure, come to think of it, whether that might not actually be worse. 'Will Angus be coming with us?' she asked as casually as she could. Not casually enough, though—he laughed and put an arm round her shoulder in jocular fashion saying, 'No, no, I'm afraid not. Can't you bear to part with me? Never mind, it's only a week, and I shall be at the conference on Saturday.'

When the meeting was over they took her out to lunch, and she began to long to be alone. It was like a conspiracy to keep her from being able to sort herself out, for after the lunch when she finally made it back to her hotel, she found a message there for her to go straight round to Maurice's office. Wearily she dragged herself off.

'My God, what have they been doing to you?' he asked at once, shoving her without ceremony into a chair.

'Oh, nothing, Maurice. I've got the blues.'

'Ah, yes, things catching up with you?' Maurce said sympathetically.

'You might say so,' she said. 'What did you want me for?'

'To talk, but I won't bother you if you're feeling miserable. You didn't talk any business last night?' he asked anxiously. Jennie managed a smile.

'No, that was the one thing we didn't get round to doing. Don't worry, I haven't been walking across your wicket.'

'Sorry?'

'Cricketing allusion, Maurice. You wouldn't understand. Has anyone spoken to you?'

'About the new contract? Oh, yes, several people, but it's all at the sounding-out stage still. I'm giving everyone a hint that someone else is interested. When they're all at fever pitch, that's the time to move in for the kill.'

Jennie sorted dazedly through the mixture of metaphors. 'Who am I going to end up with?' she asked.

'Firmans, of course, but they mustn't be allowed to know that. I want them to think they'll lose you, even despite this trip. Have they told you about that, by the way?'

'Oh, yes, we've gone over the itinerary.'

'Someone up there likes you, my dear,' Maurice said. 'I don't know who's had a word with whom, but I had a messenger came over this afternoon with a note and a very nice little cheque for you.'

'A cheque?'

'Yes—that's what I wanted to see you for. And the note—very delicately expressed, I call it—says that owing to your circumstances they thought perhaps your wardrobe wouldn't stand the strain of the publicity tour and they hoped you might find some advance expenses useful.'

'They sent me a cheque to buy some clothes?'

'They didn't want you to buy a walnut cupboard with brass handles, that's not what they mean by wardrobe. You're being very slow this afternoon, my darling. Here you are. Now are you going to be able to cash it, or do you want me to handle it for you?'

'No, it's all right, Maurice. I've got an account in London. It is very kind of them. I think I'll go and walk about the shops.'

Maurice looked at her with his head on one side. 'You want to tell me what's happened, just telephone me. And if I've gone home, you can call me at home. Don't forget Mary says you should come over any time, so if you feel lonely tonight—'

'Thanks, Maurice. You're a friend.'

Maurice smiled wryly. 'That's one word for it,' he said.

CHAPTER NINE

JENNIE LOVED to travel, and of all forms of travel she loved trains best. They travelled first-class, of course, which was heaven, except that they started off too early for them to have lunch on the train, which would have made it perfect. She got on well with Toby and Margie, and by the time they arrived in York she had told them much of her life story.

Perhaps it was as well to get into practice. On arrival in the city they were met by a car and were driven straight to the local radio studios where, having been given one of the most beastly cups of coffee she had ever been obliged to drink, she was taken into a studio and sat down opposite a young man with curly eyelashes and the puggily-handsome kind of face that was fashionable on shows like 'Top of the Pops'; the sort of face that inevitably belongs to someone called either Dave or Steve.

'Hi,' he said nervously. 'I'm Dave Bernard.'

'Well of course you are,' she said resignedly. He looked gratified that she should know him, and smiled even more nervously. It was at that point that she recognised that the nervousness was professional.

'Now, Jennie—you don't mind if I call you Jennie?' He didn't wait for her to answer. 'The scene is this—we'll just run through a few of the kind of questions I'm going to ask you, and then we'll record. I want you just to sit here nice and relaxed—smoke if you like—'

'I'm not all that hot, actually,' Jennie murmured. He did a creditable double-take but hurried on without other acknowledgement.

'But please try not to move about in your seat or touch anything on the table because the microphone—this is the microphone here—' he warned her generously; Jennie's astonished 'No!' remained internal—'will pick up any little sound and magnify it like crazy. Okay? Then when you've got the general idea we'll do the recording. You'll see a red light come on over there, and as long as that red light's on we'll be recording. Okay?'

'Okay,' she agreed. 'As long as you don't ask me what makes me write. That's one question I've never managed to get topsides of.'

'Right,' he said. 'Now then, Jennie—you've written quite a few books, haven't you—'

He asked her a few questions and then turned towards the glass box which ran the whole width of one end of the room, and which Jennie, fishing about in her general knowledge stores, decided was the control room.

'What's she like for levels?' Dave asked. There was a click and then a voice came over a loudspeaker like something out of 1984. 'Okay, but somebody was touching the table.'

Dave turned back to Jennie and relayed the message as if she were deaf.

'Your voice is okay, but I think you were touching the table. The mikes are very sensitive—'

'Yes, all right, I won't move.' She was becoming impatient now.

'We'll record now, then,' Dave said to the box. There was a countdown on the white-faced clock with the red sweep hand, and then the light went on in the corner and Dave stitched a smile across his face and introduced the programme or piece or whatever it was.

'Jennie Savage is known to thousands of readers as the

author of *The Way of the Eagle*. She's in York today promoting her new book in the same series, *The Eagle Flies*, and I invited her to come into the studio to talk to me. Hi, Jennie!'

Oh well, Jennie thought, I have to play. 'Hi, Dave,' she responded brightly.

'Jennie, tell me,' he said, his voice doing the equivalent of a friendly lean across the table, 'just what is it that makes you write?'

On the second attempt they got it done, and Jennie was astonished to discover that what she had actually recorded was a three-minute interview. It had felt like half an hour. Of course, being used to judging length by written words, she had no idea how many spoken words could be crammed into a small space, and she felt extremely jaded.

'What next?' she asked Toby as they came out into the sunshine. 'I feel like a piece of string.'

'Nothing too exacting. An hour signing copies at Shiels, the bookshop, and then lunch with the trade at the Grey Rooms. Here's the car.'

'I must say I'm impressed with the organisation,' Jennie said as she climbed in. 'Cars waiting everywhere—no hold-ups.'

'That's what I'm here for,' Toby said, touching her arm. She glanced at him and smiled, thinking that he was really rather attractive in a derivative way.

'I'm nervous about this signing business.'

'No need to be. It isn't strenuous.'

'But what do I say to them?'

'On the whole nothing. They'll mostly be too nervous, and if they do speak, they will want to tell you things. Haven't you ever seen the Queen doing walkabouts? All the people there tell her about themselves, and she nods and smiles. They don't really expect her to say anything—she's too high up.'

'Oh,' said Jennie, pondering this. 'And what happens if no one turns up at all?'

'Then you'll have nothing to worry about at all, will you?'

In fact there was quite a crowd at the shop, and Jennie had her first taste of being, however briefly, a celebrity. The crowd only knew she was the celebrity, though, by the fact that the manager of the shop came out to meet her and shake her hand, and she distinctly heard two waiting women say as she passed, 'Oh, is that her? Not a bit like her photo, is she?'

'Well they never are, are they?' the other one, replied.

A table had been set up just inside the door, covered with red and blue crepe paper, and on it a pile of copies of *The Eagle Flies* plus the counter display material. The advertising posters were pinned like a modesty flap to the front of the table, and there was a dump-bin full of more copies on either side. One thing that was missing however was a chair, and Jennie supposed she would have to sign standing up—give them a good look at her, she thought.

The hour went amazingly quickly, and Toby was right about not having to talk. Those people who had been waiting queued up with their copies, the manager handed her his fountain pen, and she began. Some of the customers spoke to her, saying things like 'Could you put "To Sharon", please. It's for my little girl', or 'I just want to say how much I liked your last one', or 'When's the next one coming out?' but most of them simply smiled shyly at her and handed the book over. One or two, she noticed with grim amusement, inspected the signature with grave suspicion as they walked away, wondering presumably how they could tell it was authentic and whether it had been worth queueing ten minutes for.

At last the manager gave her hand the farewell shake, and she was escorted almost lovingly out into the car. There she collapsed against the cushions, rubbing her hand.

'What now?' she said. 'I'm shattered.'

'I don't suppose you fancy a drink, do you?' Toby asked.

'You never said a better thing. Where?'

'Oh, I know a lovely little pub down by the river—'

'Toby, stop teasing her,' Margie said. 'Sorry, Jen, but it's an official one. The Grey Rooms are only just round the corner now. We'll have a few drinks with members of the trade, and then go in to lunch. Just carry on the way you've been doing—you're doing fine. Smile, be jolly, that sort of thing. The big thing with the trade is they've got to remember you, so you can even be a bit outrageous if you like. Just so that you stand out from the crowd.'

'Who are the people I'll be meeting?'

'Oh, reps and wholesalers and managers of bookshops and people from trade mags and those sort of types. Salt of the earth.'

'Never mind,' Jennie said, 'as long as I can get outside a couple of gins and tonics in the next ten minutes I'll survive.'

'I don't like the way you said never mind,' Margie said. 'I really meant it when I said salt of the earth.'

'She believed you,' Toby said. 'That's the trouble.'

Jennie enjoyed that part of the day. With a couple of drinks to restore her sense of proportion, she had great fun talking about herself—who doesn't like to talk about themselves?—and being flattered and flirted with by the reps, and telling them and being told by them jokes of varying degrees of respectability. The lunch was no better and no worse than she expected—the sort of food one gets at a hotel when they're catering for large numbers—and she was sat next to Toby on one side which gave her someone interesting to talk to when the conversation got dull. There was a photographer or two wandering about taking pictures with a flash gun and Toby said they were from local papers.

Then after lunch they were on the move again, by train and then hired car, for Richmond, which they reached just after five. Jennie fell in love with the town at once. It was a collection of pretty grey stone houses clustered round an old cobbled market square, and brooded over by the great mass of the castle keep. Its slopes ran down to one of the prettiest rivers she had ever seen, and beyond it the green and wooded and hilly country spread away to blue distances.

They were booked into the King's Head Hotel, which was on the market square and was evidently an old coaching inn.

It was very comfortable, and when they had been to their rooms and freshened up, they went downstairs for a cup of tea and to meet the BBC crew who were going to film them for the local roundabout programme. The Beeb types seemed very professional, if rather loud and constantly looking over their shoulders to see if people were noticing them. They all trotted across to the castle, and there Jennie spent a pleasant couple of hours walking about the ruins with the BBC presenter being filmed against this or that view, and talking about her book. The sun was setting slowly in a golden glory, throwing wonderful lights on the stones, picking out the clumps of yellow wallflowers that grew here and there in the ruins, and reflecting off the river below them. It would all look lovely on colour television, Jennie thought.

When they were finished and packing up their gear, Toby came across to her and patted her arm consolingly.

'Tired?' he questioned.

'No, not at all,' she said, sagging. 'What have I got to do now?'

'Nothing. You're all through for the day. Now we go back to the hotel and get something to eat and then go to bed.'

Jennie raised an eyebrow.

'To get an early night, I mean,' Toby elucidated swiftly.

'Oh,' Jennie said. He grinned.

'Did I detect the slightest hint of disappointment there?'

'You keep your mind on your job,' she said, giving him a little push. They walked back slowly through the gathering dusk to the hotel, and separated to go to their rooms to wash. Jennie was just debating whether to change into a pair of old jeans, or whether she still needed to keep up appearances, when there was a knock on her door.

'It's open,' she called. 'Come in.'

The door opened, and Angus Mitchell came in and stood just inside the door looking more devastatingly handsome even than she had remembered. Her heart did a number of uncertain things like an apprentice acrobat, but she said in a remarkably steady voice, 'Hello, Angus. What are you doing here?'

'Cancel all previous arrangements,' he said. 'I'm taking you out to dinner.'

'Out? Don't you mean at the hotel?'

'Not at the hotel,' he said firmly. Jennie thought of the empty open countryside all around them.

'Angus,' she said reasonably, 'it's nearly eight o'clock.'

'It's all right. It's a restaurant in the town. Discreet, pleasant, and the food they serve is actually edible. You don't need to change—you look lovely just as you are.'

'That sounded too slick to be genuine,' Jennie said peevishly. He crossed to her and stroked her hair.

'There, there,' he said. 'You're tired and hungry and you need a drink. I understand. Come on, little one, trust your uncle Angus.'

'What about Toby and Margie?'

'I've told them,' he said. A smile pushed past Jennie's defences.

'Just like that,' she murmured. 'I'll bet they didn't argue.'

'You lose your bet. Do you think I'd employ yes-men?'

'Yes.'

'There you are, you see—even you argue with me.'

Jennie whimpered. 'Stop, I'm not up to this.'

'I've already said that. Take my arm, child, and we'll go. It's only a five-minute walk, and the fresh air will give you an appetite.'

'I've got an appetite and I've had fresh air all afternoon. Just get me to a nice stuffy table and some jolly unhealthy alcohol.'

'Right. Come on then.'

Five minutes later they were seated at a corner table in a restaurant whose décor was so discreet it could hardly be said to exist. The tables were lit by candles only, so that even after your eyes became accustomed to the dark you could see nothing beyond the circle of your own table except the occasional blur of a candlelit face as someone leaned forward in the course of an intimate conversation.

'Will you let me order for you?' Angus said, when the

waiter brought the enormous card menus. Jennie nodded, only too glad not to have to make a choice, and Angus waved the menus away and ordered in rapid French which was as innocent of accent as his English. The waiter brought two martinis, and then they were left alone for a while. Jennie looked at Angus across the table, and thought how beautiful he looked by candlelight. It was nice to be here with him, although it would have been better if there had been a little more light, for it was too dark for anyone else to see them and think what a wonderful person she must be to be dining with such a beautiful man.

'It's all very well,' Angus said after a while, 'sitting there looking beautiful by candlelight, but you should speak from time to time as well.'

'Angus,' she said, and he sighed.

'By the tone of your voice I won't like it,' he said.

'Angus, what are you doing here?'

'Don't be silly. I came to see you,' he said.

She shook her head. 'It's an awfully long way. You could have had dinner cheaper at home.'

Angus considered. 'All right, do you want the real reason, or the official reason?'

'The official reason will do,' she said.

'I have to be at the Glasgow Book Fair tomorrow, so I travelled up overnight so as to make an early start there tomorrow.'

'I thought the Fair was on Wednesday.'

'Tuesday and Wednesday. You're going to the second day.'

'Oh.'

A pause. 'Don't you want to know the real reason as well?' he asked. Jennie smiled wickedly.

'No.'

'You really are a demon. You don't give me any encouragement.'

'Encouragement?' she raised an eyebrow. 'Angus, you're a married man.'

'That's why I need encouragement. If I were single I'd

manage very nicely on my own. I came all this way to see you —there you are, you see, you've got it out of me anyway.'

'The real reason?'

'Yes.'

She smiled. 'The real real reason, or the official real reason?'

He reached across the table and took her hand. It was a gesture of friendship not of seduction, and she allowed it. 'All right. Round one to you. I'll tell you later. Let's enjoy dinner. Tell me about your day.'

The first course came, served in individual earthenware pots—a marvellous mixture of seafood in a caper sauce topped with mashed potato that had been grilled crisp with cheese. It was utterly delicious. With it came a bottle of chilled rosé wine.

'Why is it rosé?' Jennie asked after the first ecstatic gulp and sip.

'It's made from the same grapes as red wine, but they take the skins out before the process is complete. It's really only a pale red wine. With red wine they leave the skins in right to the end.'

'What fascinating things you know,' she said. 'I'll use that in a book one day, when I'm writing about a suave, knowledgeable, man-of-the-world hero—'

'Having a candlelit dinner with a lovely, desirable heroine—'

'Who sees through him,' Jennie finished.

The second course was a small game-bird served whole on a slice of fried bread spread with a thick layer of paté. With it came a green salad and a bunch of grapes, the only accompaniments which would not have been too heavy for such a rich dish. They talked about books and music as they ate, then drifted on to pictures and thence by a fairly logical route to the great cities of Europe and their travels.

'There is so much I want to see,' Jennie said with a sigh. 'I seem to have wasted so much of my life in one place. When I'm travelling, I love it so much that I feel betrayed if I stay in the same place two days running.'

'You must never do it again, Jennie,' Angus said seriously.

'Do what?'

'Bury yourself in a backwater tax-haven like that.'

'Well it wasn't my idea in the first place,' Jennie shrugged.

'No, I know. What ever did you marry a creep like him for?'

'Now wait a minute, you can't say that.'

'Why not? He *is* a creep.'

'You don't know Miles—' Jennie began, and Angus laughed.

'Do you?'

'Of course I do, innocent. I used to work for Cavelles.'

'I didn't know that. It seems to me that all you people in publishing go round and round like a roundabout, getting off at one place and getting back on at another. You knew Miles at Cavelles?'

'Yep. And I never liked him. Stuffy old bore. Can't think what you ever saw in him.'

'Oh, come on. He's a great writer.'

'He's not. All that boring, fiddling detail, every last damn second worked out exactly, but not a decent character anywhere in the book. And do you know why? Because he's not interested in people. He's only interested in himself, so all his characters are grey cardboard cutouts of him.' Jennie had begun to laugh at his vehemence. 'I always hated his bloody books.'

'They sell.'

'That is no criterion.'

'And *that* is heresy.'

'True.'

'He's a better writer than I am.'

'He's not.'

'He's a more successful writer than I am, and after all, Angus, what else concerns you?'

'I'll pass over that slur on my character for the moment. We'll discuss that part of it later. But as for his being more successful—that is not an unalterable feature of the universe. You and I, Jennie, are going to make your books sell better than anything he's ever dreamed of. We are going to make you a star.'

Ah, thought Jennie. I've come to it—the real reason, or rather the real, real reason.

'What's the matter?' Angus said. 'Your face has gone a shade paler.'

Jennie heaved a dramatic sigh. 'And I thought you were after my body.'

Angus looked startled. 'Aren't I?'

'No, you're after a contract.' He didn't deny or agree. 'You know, then, that Cavelles want me to sign up with them for a series?'

'I had heard something about it.'

A little crude, she thought, working on me via Miles to get me to dislike Cavelles. His comments about Miles she realised were based on justice, though exaggerated, yet she felt still the pain of his rejection of her, only half hidden below her surface professionalism. Was there something wrong with her, perhaps? Surely there must be, if he could abandon her with such ease for Bea, who, though a nice enough girl, had no particular talents.

'He loved me once, you know,' she said suddenly.

Angus shook his head and said gently, 'I don't think he ever really thought about you. If he had, he wouldn't have taken you off to Crete like that. It was not, you know, the best thing for your career. It didn't matter to him, because he's the sort who will continue to grind out one book a year of absolutely uniform quality and selling potential for ever. But you—you have far more potential than him. I wouldn't be surprised if he didn't do it deliberately to squash you. Some people can't live with competition.'

'You're contradicting yourself,' Jennie said in a small voice.

'Yes, well, nobody's perfect. Do you want anything else to eat? Or some coffee? Well then, shall we go? I feel like some fresh air after all that good food.'

Angus paid, and soon they were out in the sweet summer night. He took Jennie's hand and pulled it under the crook of his arm, and turned their footsteps away from the hotel and towards the river. Jennie did not protest. Her head was reeling, partly from tiredness, partly from wine, and partly from what they had been saying. There was a moon, riding high and white in the black liquid sky, and in the west there was still a faint luminosity from the departed sun. It was quiet, and the only sound apart from their footsteps was the eerie rushing of the river running over stones, growing louder as it flowed down the hill to the elegant old pack-bridge.

They stopped half-way across the bridge and leaned against the parapet to look. On the left, the green bank rose steeply, wooded with silver birch and willow, to the walls of the castle, silvery in the moonlight, with empty black eyes. Before them the broad river ran over a shallow, rocky bed, and as they watched here and there a fish jumped up and turned flashing silver in the air for a fly before falling back into the water with a plop. During the day Jennie could imagine the swallows swooping back and forth across the surface, screaming as they fed. On the right there was only the wood, thick and crowded with great trees all in full leaf, rising tier on tier to the sky.

Jennie sighed. 'It's so beautiful here. There's nothing, nothing, in all the world to compare with the beauty of England. Nothing has the subtlety, the quality of light, the richness, the variety. I love to travel, but now I'm home I don't ever want to go away again.'

'Now you're contradicting yourself,' Angus smiled. She turned to look at him.

'No. You know what I mean. I want to go everywhere and do everything, but I don't want to live anywhere but England. England the beautiful.'

He was like an alabaster statue, she thought, except for the blue, lively eyes, and the crest of hair that blew ever so slightly in the movement of the warm air. She saw his lips part and the gleam of a smile, and then a wave of emotion rushed over her and she found herself almost without volition in his arms, holding him like a child holding on to an adult, her face pressed against his chest. His arms tightened round her, and he—bless him—said nothing until the paroxysm was over. Then, very gently, he eased her back from him just a little, and kissed her.

The first touch of his lips made her spine kick like electricity, but after that she felt only enormous relief and uncomplicated, friendly love. It had not been him! The relief of finding out was so huge that she thought her legs would give way under her. It had not been him that came to her in the night—she could never have mistaken the mouth, though their skin smelled so alike that she could easily have thought one was the other in the dark, even now, if that was all she was going by. But the mouth—the mouth!

She drew back from him at last, and, smiling, lifted his hand and turned it over. There was a small healing cut in the palm—he really had cut his hand on a tin. She had made something out of nothing, out of her own neurotic imagination. She planted a kiss on the palm, folded the fingers over it, and gave his hand back to him. He smiled down at her with great friendliness, and she smiled back.

'Thank you for a lovely evening,' she said. He put an arm round her shoulders and they turned back towards the hotel without another word.

CHAPTER TEN

EVERYTHING MAY have been done first-class, but it didn't alter the fact that they had to set off at half-past-seven the next morning to go to Edinburgh, which is definitely a second-class time to get up. Everyone was a little out of sorts, too. Toby was cross because Angus had turned up, and he muttered in an undertone when he thought Jennie was not listening about being checked up on and not being trusted.

Jennie could not at first decide what it was that Margie was cross about, but gradually it became evident that it was something she was trying to keep from Jennie, and from there it was only a short step for a romantic novelist to discover that Margie fancied Toby but thought Toby was after Jennie. As for Jennie herself, while last night's walk with Angus had put her mind at ease about one thing, it had made her all the more sure that what she had felt happening between her and Nick was imagination. It was not surprising that a person in her position should imagine things like that, but it did not help her battered ego. She sighed, and then shook herself.

Ego be damned, she thought, whatever happened to logic? From now on—and then she laughed at herself, knowing from old experience how rarely resolves that begin with 'from now on' are kept to. Like giving up smoking, one can do it twelve times an hour. At least she was able to indulge her fancy for eating on trains: they had a marvellous breakfast—there isn't much anyone can do to spoil bacon and eggs—while the train hurtled through some glorious countryside under a pale gold early sun, which gave her ample opportunity for the loins-girding she had to do to face the day.

The day in Edinburgh was much like the day in York, except that she was able to watch herself on television back at the hotel between the afternoon and the evening engagements. She was gratified to discover how smooth she sounded.

'You're good,' Margie commented. 'See how much less nervous you are now?'

'Repetition cures all,' Jennie said. 'It's getting so bad that my brain can select the tape without actually passing through my conscious mind at all. I've had the same questions asked so often—'

'Tomorrow won't be so bad,' Toby assured her. 'Book Fair tomorrow. Not that they won't be asking the same questions, but there'll be other authors there to spread the load, and various editors and promo bods—'

'And Angus,' Margie said, with a pointed air of not being pointed about it. 'He'll take care of you, Jennie, and bring the roses back to your cheeks.'

Jennie merely raised an eyebrow at this, but Toby frowned at Margie.

'What's that supposed to mean?' he asked crossly. Margie's smile grew more fixed.

'Oh, I just had the impression that Jennie was sweet on our Angus.' She turned her gaze hastily from Toby to Jennie and went on kindly, 'It doesn't matter—most of us have to go through it. After all, he is rather stunning, isn't he?'

'I think that's an understatement,' Jennie said calmly. 'But you can put your mind at rest—strange though it may seem, he isn't my type.'

'He's everyone's type,' Margie said firmly, 'but he's devoted to his wife, so that's sucks to the rest of us.'

I wonder why, Jennie pondered, people keep warning me off people. Do I look dangerous? That was a pleasant thought. She hoped, however, that Margie and Toby would get to bed soon and clear the air.

Glasgow was only an hour from Edinburgh, so they didn't have to start out until nine. The Book Fair was being held in one of the City Chambers, and when Jennie was ushered in through the door she discovered a scene which at first reminded her irresistibly of the Fresher's Fair at her university. The hall was laid out in rows with stalls belonging to the various publishers on which they displayed advertising material and books and photographs and posters to promote their list for the coming year. Behind the stalls stood members of staff of the publishers dressed in their best, shining with anxiety and *bonhomie* and wearing large plastic badges with their name and company printed on them. It was still early and the buyers were thin on the ground and were strolling about with the superior air of so many yellow-dog-dingoes. At the Fresher's Fair it had been the various clubs and societies who had been drumming up trade, and there, as here, it was obvious by the air of prosperity hanging about the stalls which ones were the popular and successful ones.

Gradually the place filled up and from feeling like a spare prick at a wedding Jennie came to feel like a former head girl at an old girls' meeting—she never had time to finish a conversation because there was always someone else coming up to her to greet her either as an old friend or in her official capacity. There were a number of other writers there with whom she had greater or lesser acquaintance and they continually formed little knots in corners where they fell into eager discussion of royalties, sales figures, and the ins and outs of contracts. Then they would be chivvied away from each other by their respective publishers who wore the anxious air of dog-owners whose pets are sniffing each other in the street.

There were also a number of acquaintances from the trade, people in publishing and even some of the reps and wholesalers she had met in York and Edinburgh. Jennie was beginning to feel like an old hand, and it took Margie and Toby to remind her that she was here for their purposes and not for her own enjoyment. When it got to eleven o'clock the bar opened and the talk became instantly livelier. Jennie found herself remembering the Ideal Home Exhibition where you could tell which corners of the hall had licensed refreshment stalls by the amount and quality of trade the stands were doing.

They had a late and very cheerful lunch at a hotel a short walk away, and then returned to the fray for a repeat of the morning. There were various photographers around, and Jennie could only hope that if they wanted shots of her they'd take them without asking, because someone only had to point a camera at her and her face started to twitch like a dog dreaming of rabbits. She said as much to a writer friend, Pamela Fielding, who had like Jennie temporarily escaped her owners and was gossiping with her by the Firmans stand.

'I'm the same,' Pam said. 'My face muscles go into spasm and I give the most ghastly grin—what Ian Fleming always calls the rictus of death.'

'The last time Mandersons wanted a press photograph of me,' Jennie said, 'they sent me to a very well thought of professional, and he had to take a hundred and fifty exposures before he got one where I didn't look like a badly weathered gargoyle.'

Pam laughed. 'And do you know—' she began and then stopped, looking over Jennie's shoulder. 'I say, who is that absolutely divine man coming towards you?'

Jennie looked and smiled. 'Oh, that's my new owner, Pammie, Angus Mitchell. I think we're about to be split up and told to do our duty.'

'He doesn't look like a publisher. Altogether too pretty,' Pam said. Jennie agreed.

'He looks like one of those exquisite creatures who escort minor foreign royalty to private parties in Monte—' and there she stopped. Her skin stiffened up as if she'd been dipped in paste and her hair rose slightly on her scalp. Pushing through the crowds behind Angus came Nick. His face was as expressionless as a mask, but his eyes were fixed on Jennie.

'Come on, break it up, you two,' Angus said cheerfully. 'You're not here to enjoy yourselves. And you, Pam, go on back to your own stall.'

'You have the advantage of me, I'm afraid,' Pam said, trying to sound cool and distant, but being overcome by the blueness of Angus's eyes and the blackness of his curly eyelashes.

'I'm so sorry—how terribly rude of me,' Angus said. 'I know you of course, in your professional capacity. I'm Angus Mitchell—Firman and Jackson.' Pam gave him her hand. 'And this is my brother, Nick—' he repeated louder, 'I said my brother, Nick.'

Nick removed his gaze from Jennie and hastily shook hands with Pam. Pam smiled wryly and said, 'If you'll excuse me, I think I'd better be going back.' And she pressed Jennie's hand secretly with a sideways slide of her eyes towards Nick, which made Jennie blush suddenly and painfully at the implication. She squeezed Pam's hand back, which was meant to convey that Pam was mistaken and that she wasn't going to be led astray by imagination again, but there's a limit to what you can convey in a squeeze and Pam went on her way with her satisfied smirk unimpaired.

'Nice girl, Pam,' Angus said when she had gone. 'I wouldn't mind poaching her if the Bodders ever slackened their grip. Not that they're likely to—will you excuse me a moment, Jennie? I must go and sort out my staff.'

'Don't use that expression to them,' Jennie called after him in a belated attempt not to appear dumbstruck. 'It undermines their confidence.'

And then she was left alone with Nick. He was standing a foot away from her, but still her skin was crawling as if invaded by ants, and her heart was jumping about inside her in a way that made her feel either dizzy or sick, but mostly cross with herself. I won't start this silly business again, she told herself firmly, but it didn't help. She couldn't look at him. He was standing slightly slumped like someone with their hands in their pockets, although his hands weren't and his face was absolutely impassive, as if he had been brought here against his will and was resigned to it.

When the silence had endured for some minutes Jennie thought it was stupid and looked up at him. It was a bad moment, and better got over. She blushed again, meeting the eyes of the man who had made love to her and, she imagined, led her to make a fool of herself. What was he thinking? Did she betray her feelings, and was he inwardly despising her, or laughing at her, or intending to prey on her? There was absolutely nothing to be gained from his expression. She said at last, 'Well, what are you doing here?'

He was so long answering she thought he was not going to, which would have left her with the problem of what to say next. But at last he said in a carefully neutral voice, 'Oh, I happened to have some spare time, and Angus wanted company. So I let myself be dragged along here.'

'It seems a long way to be dragged,' Jennie said.

'I like Glasgow,' he said, as if that were an answer. 'And there's a free dinner to be had out of it.'

'Is there?'

'At the Caledonian tonight. Courtesy of Firman and Jackson. Aren't you invited?'

'I don't know. Nobody's said so. I suppose I must be, since that's where we're staying. The dear old Cally—it brings back memories.'

It would have made conversation infinitely easier if he had picked up the cue, but he seemed to conduct conversation according to his own rules, and he said instead, 'You seem very much at home here.'

'Here at the Fair, or here in Glasgow?' He didn't answer again, and she added, 'Or here in this conversation?'

One eyebrow went up, Spock-style, and the faintest gleam of humanity showed for a moment in his flat eyes. But all he replied was, 'Here at the Fair.'

'After—what?—seven-and-a-half hours of it, I should,' Jennie said. 'And besides, there are a lot of people I know here. It's rather pleasant, having my identity reaffirmed—in Crete there were so few people I knew.'

'I don't know anyone here,' he said, looking round briefly and then back at Jennie. 'Except you.'

Jennie almost said 'And you don't actually know me' but it would have been sophistry, and dangerous. Instead she found herself babbling on.

'It's good to be in a place where I'm known in my writing persona and not in my wifely one. At least no one here talks about Miles to me. I can actually forget for long periods that I'm Jennie-the-abandoned-wife and concentrate on being Jennie-the-successful-writer.'

Babble or not, it seemed to spark something off in him. His face took on one or two curves of life, and she could see that he was gathering himself to say something when Angus came back with Tony and Margie.

'Closing up time,' Angus said. 'I think we ought to go over to the hotel. If we don't make a move nobody else will. Drinks in the conference room, and then dinner. Toby, you take Nick and Jennie over, will you, and Margie, you come with me and we'll round up the others.'

'So I am invited,' Jennie said to Toby as they began to make their way to the door. Toby smiled at her his charming, lopsided Paul McCartney smile, and placed a gentle hand on her arm.

'Don't be so bloody stupid,' he said.

At the hotel he went up to get a round of drinks, and Jennie drifted after him.

'Listen, Toby, I feel a bit at a loss in all this crowd.'

'You?' he said. 'Our star turn?'

'Never mind,' she said. 'When I had a press conference given for my first book with Mandersons, as soon as the reporters had got the details they wanted, everyone abandoned me and dashed for the bar and I was left feeling extremely stupid. I didn't even get a drink that day.'

'Shame!'

'So please, will you be very kind and stick with me and look after me?'

Toby glowed. 'Of course I will. Apart from being my job, it'll be my pleasure.'

The plan worked quite well. Soon other people from the Fair were pushing into the room, and it was easy to get separated from the person you were standing next to. Toby, forewarned, kept a hand on her arm and remained with her, while Nick was gradually edged away. Safe, Jennie thought. By a bit of judicious hustling she managed to get herself and Toby seated at the far end of the table from Angus and Nick at dinner, and then she allowed herself to relax. Imagination or not, her reactions to him were too extreme to risk exposing herself to his radiation.

Jennie and Toby got on well together. They were about of an age, their backgrounds and education were similar, and they shared a sense of humour, both liking the absurd and the witty. Whether or not it was professional she did not know, but he also had an eager way of asking questions and an interested way of listening to the answers which led her to talk about herself and not feel she was being boring. At the end of the meal he knew a lot more about her than she knew about him, but she did at least know that he was unmarried and unattached and that there was nothing formal between him and Margie. Jennie had detected some signs of physical warmth too, and she was beginning to wonder pleasantly if they might end up in bed together, a thought she found more than agreeable.

People were beginning to get up and drift around, some going out to the bar for more drinks, some merely changing places to talk to different people. It made Jennie feel vulnerable again, and so she suggested to Toby that they go into the bar, and he agreed with alacrity. The bar was even more crowded than it had been before dinner, and Jennie soon saw why—everyone who had been at the Book Fair had gathered there for drinks. Toby went up to the bar, and Jennie was instantly seized round the waist from behind and a kiss was planted on her ear that made her head ring.

'Oh, it's you,' she said with relief when she looked round and saw Quin West. 'What are you doing here?'

'What do you mean? What a silly question. What I want to know is, why are you alone? Have you slipped your leash, dear heart, or are you the Judas goat, left out for unwary editors like me?'

'None of those,' Jennie laughed. 'My present keeper has just gone to get me a drink.'

'Ah, the little dark-haired boy I saw you with earlier? Yes, but what about the Generalissimo? He must feel very secure of you if he dares leave you alone like this. Doesn't he realise someone else will snap you up if he doesn't?'

'I escaped,' Jennie said. 'I had a kind of feeling I was meant to sit at the top of the table, so I hastily grabbed myself a place below the salt.'

Quin shook his head sadly. 'He's losing his grip if he just let you. No, no, I can't believe yer actual Angus would be so slack. He must be really sure of you. What's he been doing to you?' He stooped and stared at Jennie's face curiously. 'He hasn't been sleeping with you? No, it can't be that. I know—he's thrown you his brother.' Jennie tried hard to show nothing in her face, but Quin straightened up, smiling triumphantly. 'Yes, that it—that's the bait, isn't it, darling? A good idea, though a bit unscrupulous considering you're in the throes of a divorce.'

'Quin, you're talking nonsense, and malicious nonsense at that.'

'No, I'm not, darling,' Quin said, looking surprised. 'Listen, lassie, we'd do very nearly anything to get what we want. Don't you realise you're a hot property at the moment? Three of us trying to sign you, and until you're signed, all's fair in war, including love.'

'Well I haven't been offered that,' Jennie said firmly. 'Don't you think, in any case, that the brother might have something to say about it?'

Quin smiled. 'I don't think he'd mind too much. Who would? If you fancied me, now—'

Then he burst out laughing, and Jennie, turning a shade redder, realised that the whole thing had been a practical joke. Quin wiped tears from his eyes as Toby came back holding two drinks and looking partly puzzled and partly disapproving.

'Oh, Jen, you'll be the death of me,' he said, putting an arm round her. 'I'm sorry, I shouldn't have led you on like that, but really—'

'It was in bad taste,' Jennie said, trying not to laugh.

'All the best jokes are,' he said. He smiled down at her affectionately. 'Do you forgive me? Come on, we're old friends—nothing's bad between friends, is it?'

'Don't do it again, or I'll tell Jim,' Jennie said. When he had gone, she took her drink from Toby and thanked him. 'You see what happens when you leave me alone for a moment? Next time I'm coming up to the bar with you.'

'Suits me,' he said. They fell into a pleasant conversation again, and were making up the old ground nicely when they were interrupted, rather tempestuously by Margie.

'You're not supposed to be skulking here, Jennie, you're supposed to be circulating,' she said, grabbing Jennie's arm in a hard grip that suggested she'd had a little too much to drink. 'Now then, who can I introduce you to? Oh yes—there's someone you must meet. Come on!' And she dragged Jennie away so forcibly that she had no chance to resist, and Toby had no chance to stop her. Margie pulled her through the crowds to the side of the room and then dropped her in a space and darted off again. Jennie looked round for escape, but not quickly enough, for Margie came back dragging a very unwilling Nick by the arm.

'You simply *must* meet Nicholas Mitchell,' Margie said, dropping Nick in the same space opposite Jennie. 'He's our Angus's brother.'

'We've met,' Jennie said blankly, staring at him. He gave the faintest hint of a smile and shrug, as if to say, *this is inevitable.* She turned to Margie. 'You must know that—we were standing together at the Book Fair when you came up with Angus.'

Now Margie looked blank. 'Were you? Oh well, never mind. You two must look after each other. Excuse me—'

And she was gone. Nick watched her go and then turned back very slowly—perhaps unwillingly?—to Jennie.

'What was all that about?' he asked. Jennie shrugged.

'I think she's after Toby, the young man who was looking after me. I expect this was the only way she could feel sure of detaching me from him.'

'Why—are you keen?'

'I just didn't want to find myself left high and dry with no one to talk to,' Jennie explained. 'I asked him to take care of me, that's all.'

'I see.' He thought for a moment. 'Well, will I do? At least I have the advantage of being an acquaintance—I won't say friend.'

'Won't you? Why not?'

He looked away from her, and his mouth turned down bitterly. 'I don't think there can ever be friendship between a man and a woman.'

'What an extraordinary thing to say,' Jennie said. 'Of course there can. Why not?'

'Because sex gets in the way. You can't have any kind of relationship without the sexual thing intervening, and once it does, there are no rules. You treat each other with—' he paused as if looking for a word —'dishonour,' he finished. It wasn't she realised, that he hadn't known the word, but because he felt it so old-fashioned and absurd a notion that he had to prepare for it with a pause. 'And there's no friendship without honour.'

'What did she do to you,' Jennie said suddenly, 'to make you so bitter?'

Now he looked at her with faint surprise. 'You knew about her?'

She shook her head. 'I surmise her. Who was it—your wife?'

'I grew up with her,' he said, and the words seemed to burst out of him painfully as if he had been holding them back for a long time. 'We were cousins. We played together as children. We had a tree house we built together, and there was a hole in the tree where we kept secret things. We used to put letters to each other in it, like a post-box. It was our secret—no one else knew about it. It was like that all the time as we grew up, the two of us against the world. I trusted her automatically.'

'And then you got married?'

'When we both finished university. It seemed that was the only thing to do. The obvious thing. It was all right at first, we just went on as we always had, except that we were—lovers, as well.' The hesitation over that word was of a different sort; it wasn't quite the word he wanted.

'And now she's fallen in love with someone else,' Jennie said.

'A boy,' he said, sourly. 'A boy half her age.'

'And you feel betrayed.'

'I *am* betrayed.'

'And now you're wondering how many other men she betrayed you with that you don't know about.'

He stared at her in astonishment. 'How do you know that?'

She smiled at him, almost laughed, and saw his face beginning to respond. 'Oh, Nick,' she said, 'I'm a writer. She probably didn't, you know, any more than you did. People are pretty much the same underneath it all. The differences are mostly on the surface.'

'*You* can say that?' he said. She raised an enquiring eyebrow, and he looked away uncomfortably. 'You know what I mean.'

'Perhaps. Perhaps you ought to tell me.'

He looked at her speculatively for a long time, and then shook his head. 'No. Not now.'

'Then we'd better talk about something else,' she said. She felt strangely at ease with him, as if there was nothing she couldn't say, nothing she need fear. *Why was that*, she asked herself. *Because I want nothing from him? Not true. Then, because I hope for nothing from him? More difficult to determine. Because—because I think I understand him. Because I think I'm sure he means me no harm.*

'Let me get you another drink, before we start,' he said. 'I need a refill.'

'All right,' she said, 'but I'm coming with you to the bar. I don't want to get separated again.'

He looked down at her in surprise, and then smiled fully for the first time, lighting up his face and making her knees go weak all over again. He reached out for her hand and when she gave it, drew it through his arm and pressed it against his ribs. 'I won't let you get separated,' he said.

Having gained the bar they stayed there—there seemed no point in leaving it when they'd have to get back to it sooner or later. They were left there unmolested, and gradually the numbers thinned out as people went home or to private parties or merely to bed. Angus found them there later, with Margie in tow.

'Toby's gone to bed,' Angus said, explaining without knowing it why Margie looked so cross. 'We're going now, but you two stay here. No need to leave if you're enjoying yourselves. Have your drinks put down to my room number if you like. Goodnight.'

He left them abruptly, and Jennie and Nick surveyed each other speculatively.

'Nothing like being subtle,' Jennie said.

'No,' he said. 'That *was* nothing like being subtle. I'm sorry. Do you want another drink?'

'I think so,' she said.

'Because what I think we should do is take the bastard up on his offer. I think we ought to order a bottle of whisky on him, and take it up to my room to drink. It'll be more comfortable.'

Jennie hesitated, and he looked impatient.

'Oh, come on,' he said. 'I mean it unambiguously. It will be more comfortable. I'm offering you a drink, that's all.'

Jennie shrugged consent, but as she followed him to the lift she wondered whether that didn't make it worse. Nobody likes to think they're resistible.

CHAPTER ELEVEN

NICK'S ROOM was on the first floor, which should have been warning enougn to Jennie, who had only ever been as low as the third. It was practically a suite, with a sitting-room end containing a sofa and two armchairs, a coffee table, a television, and a writing-desk and chair, as well as a fridge stocked with mixers and ice; a bathroom *en suite*; and at the other end a large double bed with a battery of controls built into the bedside table that would do everything from opening and closing the curtains to summoning the fire brigade.

They sat down on the sofa. While Nick busied himself pouring the whisky into the glasses he had obtained for them, Jennie kicked off her shoes tucking her feet under her, feeling that the more at home she made herself the better she would be able to cope with the situation. The problem was, knowing what the situation was. Having from the start done everything he could to put her off Nick, Angus seemed now to be throwing them together, and she couldn't account for it. Was it perhaps as Quin had said, though he retracted it as a joke? Was he trying to keep Jennie happy until she signed the contract? That did seem rather extreme; but perhaps Quin was trying to warn her, disguising his warning but giving it all the same.

Nick passed her a glass of whisky then sat back at his end of the sofa and raised his glass to her.

'Cheers,' she said, and drank. She could not keep her eyes from him. It was like trying not to look at a television screen in a darkened room; but he seemed to be able to keep up a steady gaze with eyes as flat as the soles of his boots, while she felt burned, discomfited, out of countenance. Her heart was still thudding erratically, and the palms of her hands were sweaty. He did things to her; that part wasn't imagination. Even if it was only the old adam poking his head up through the veneer of sophistication, there was no denying that she *had* a reaction to him.

'Well,' he said at last, 'what shall we talk about?' He sounded ironic, and Jennie countered that by taking him literally.

'Anything except my work,' she said. 'I've talked about that non-stop for three days and I've got another two days to go.'

'Are you enjoying the trip?'

'Pretty much. Are you?'

'What trip?'

'All right—what are you doing here?'

'I told you.'

'Yes, but really. You don't come five hundred miles for dinner, just like that.'

'I do,' he said firmly. 'All right then, I came to see you. Is that what you want to hear?'

'Don't talk rot,' she said angrily. 'I don't "want" to hear anything. If I ask you a question it's because I want an answer. No, not *an* answer—I want *the* answer.'

'You're a rare woman, then.'

'I've no time for deviousness. There's enough difficulty to be encountered in life without adding to it.' She drained her glass abruptly, angry to find herself shaking, and the hot, neat spirit burned her throat and brought tears to her eyes. The feeling told her she was a lot closer to crying than she had realised. In another moment, she thought, I shall either tell him all my troubles, or ask him something extremely embarrassing. He was watching her, not turning his eyes away from her distress. Suddenly he put his glass down on the table with the delicately precise movement of a chess-player, and the sharp click of it sounded loud in a room that contained only the sound of their breathing.

'Jennie,' he said, reaching for her.

'No,' she said, struggling harder with tears.

'Don't be a fool,' he said, taking her in his arms and pulling her towards him. She resisted, trying to turn her face away, trying not to see his eyes.

'No,' she said again. 'It isn't fair. It isn't fair!'

'Why should it be fair?' he asked, and holding her with one arm, took her face with his other hand and turned it. His fingers were long and strong, and resistance hurt her. She had to let him pull her face round to his. The tears were escaping her eyes now, trickling down her cheeks. His face was close to hers, so close it looked blurred, all except his shining eyes. He put out the tip of his tongue and licked the tears neatly from her face, and then ran it across her lips, and then the shining eyes were blotted out abruptly as he closed them and pressed his mouth down on to hers. The resistance went out of her in one shudder, and she yielded against him, her lips parting for his tongue and her hands going up to his neck.

He kissed her for a long time, very still, and then with a sigh he stood up and drew her across to the bed. She went with him, as helpless as a febrile child, and stood shivering slightly as he took off her clothes, folding them neatly on a chair behind him. When she was naked, clothed only in her hair, he kissed her once, quietly, on the forehead, and then opened the bed and put her gently in it. Then he stood where she could see him and took off his own clothes, piling them with the same fastidiousness on top of hers.

She watched him from the pillow, not afraid, exactly, but apprehensive. She could not then analyse her fears; afterwards it came to her that she was apprehensive as to how he would make her feel. When he was naked he stood for a moment looking down at her. His body was not tanned, but naturally dark-skinned, olive perhaps was the word; slender and straight, unspoilt. The hair on his chest was straight and silky and black; thin, fine hair. The skin on the insides of his arms was very white, and the veins showed blue, like rivers on a map. His penis was not erect. His face seemed so familiar and unthreatening that he might have been a brother or a father, except that there would have been more to fear from a brother or father.

He pulled back the covers and got in beside her, and drew her carefully on to his shoulder. She did not resist, but he must have sensed her apprehension, for he asked, 'What's the matter?'

'I'm afraid,' she admitted. He kissed her forehead, and then moved his lips down with small kisses to her mouth and spoke into it, punctuating his words with kisses.

'That's as it should be. I'm afraid too.'

There was no more speech then. They spoke only with their bodies. Jennie pressed her face to him and drew in lungfuls of the smell of his skin while her blind fingers explored the continent of his body seeking God knows what reassurance, but finding it. His skin was like silk, his limbs hard as jewel. Her hands knew the shape of his skull, the line of his jaw. The weight of his body was familiar, his possession of her was both agony and relief, expected and known and yet as alien as violation. Something in her did not want to yield, *would* not yield, and the yielding, though it was pain, was a wonderful relief.

Time seemed suspended. They made long, slow love that seemed to extend itself into a sphere where there was no time, only duration, and their bodies performed a slow ritual dance that went on for ever without repetition. Even when she reached a climax with him, it was slow and quiet, easing over her like a great Atlantic comber turning over on a beach, not the sudden and violent thing it had always been before.

Tenderly he stroked her hair away from her brow and kissed it, and looked down at her, propping himself on one elbow. He wiped a faint dew of sweat away from under her eyes.

'Sweat or tears?' he said. He licked his fingers and smiled.

'Both would be salt. You have a look about you—as if you were bruised.'

'I never saw such eyes as yours,' she said in response, not in reply. His eyes shone preternaturally. They were gold, quite gold, but the irises were textured like woven gold cloth, and there were flecks in them of darker gold, almost the colour of autumn bracken.

'Can you sleep?' he asked. 'If I turn out the light will you sleep?'

'I think so,' she said. At his words she grew drowsy. Was that autosuggestion, or obedience? 'You won't go away?'

'No, of course not,' he said. He reached up and switched off the bedside light, and in the darkness lay down and drew her, as he had before, on to his shoulder, closed his arms about her, and was instantly asleep. Jennie lay awake for some time, but she was unable to think of anything at all. All that happened in her consciousness was feeling, the sensation she had of being home. Then she was asleep, without any awareness that she was going.

Someone kissed her. She stirred and murmured, and then was instantly awake, remembering where she was and what had happened. Nick was sitting on the edge of the bed beside her, fully dressed, washed and shaved.

'It's all right,' he said, 'it's still early. I have to go, but you can go back to sleep.'

She looked up at him mutely, wondering what had happened between them. His face looked less familiar this morning, not less dear, but less accessible. As if he divined her trouble, he said with a reassuring smile,

'When you get back to London, don't go back to the hotel. It's go dreary. I have a large flat. It belongs to a friend who's gone away for the summer. Come and stay there until you find a place of your own to live.' She said nothing. 'It's what I'm doing,' he pointed out. 'Look, I've put the address and the front door key in this envelope. You can come and go as you wish.'

Still she said nothing. It wasn't so much the giving in that was difficult, as finding the words to acknowledge it. He put the envelope down on the bedside table again and looked at her with enormous sympathy.

'Au moins,' he said quietly, 'tu n'as rien à perdre.'

'No,' she said resignedly. 'Nothing at all.'

The flat was in one of those enormous, elegant Georgian houses between Earl's Court and Kensington. Jennie did not go there until late Sunday morning, for she had felt it more advisable to stay at the hotel for the night after the final dinner-reception, and even as she climbed the stairs with her meagre luggage in her hand she was doubting the wisdom of what she was doing. It was all very well falling in love with someone, even going to bed with them; but arriving on their doorstep with all your worldly goods in your hand—that was surely laying yourself open. That it wasn't his doorstep entirely didn't help.

Feeling hesitant she rang the doorbell rather than using the key, but there was no answer, and between surprise and apprehension she let herself in. The place had the shining cleanness of a house tended by a daily cleaner. An enormous hall led off into enormous rooms with Adam fireplaces and moulded ceilings and panelled shutters for the windows and service bells that rang in the kitchen. Jennie put down her bags in the hall and explored carefully. She discovered four bedrooms and two bathrooms, and in the second bathroom was shaving gear on the shelf over the basin. It might have been evidence of Nick's occupancy, or on the other hand it might have been a spare set left by the owner. Did men have spare sets of shaving gear? Jennie pondered the point. There didn't seem any reason why they shouldn't, but on the other hand, she had the feeling that men regarded their razors with the same kind of quirky partisanship that trumpet-players had towards their mouthpieces. She would have to ask some of her male friends, in case it ever came in useful in a book. Catching herself 'researching' she smiled and was going back to the hall when she heard the front door opening.

She rounded the corner of the passage at the same moment as Nick came in through the front door, holding under his arm a fat bundle which could only be the *Sunday Times* and *Observer*. They stopped and regarded each other with probably about equal shock.

'Hullo,' he said at last. 'You found your way then?'

'Yes,' Jennie said, simply.

He was not smiling, not even looking particularly pleased to see her, and she wondered if his invitation had been the kind of spur-of-the-moment suggestion that wears off once you're out of sight of each other. He was simply staring at her with his expressionless expression. Then he grew brisk, removed his gaze, and walked past her down the side passage to the kitchen saying, 'I've just been out to get the Sundays. One thing I'll really look forward to when I get my own place again is having the papers delivered. There's something barbaric about having to go out and get them. I was just going to make some coffee. Would you like some? Have you breakfasted?'

'It's past eleven,' she said by way of an answer as she followed him.

'Is it?' he said indifferently. 'But then it's Sunday. Sit down there, out of the way, while I get the coffee on. You like coffee, I take it? Or do you prefer tea?'

'Coffee, since it's this late. First thing I prefer tea.'

He turned and gave her the first smile, though it was only a faint and tentative one. 'So do I. We have something in common then.'

'It's rather nice, not knowing preferences like that. There comes a stage—' She had been going to say there comes a stage in an affair when you don't need to ask how the other person takes their tea; but she realised as she began that she really didn't want to finish that sentence. Nick didn't seem to notice that she had stopped. He busied himself round an elaborate-looking coffee-maker that might have needed a licence to drive. Jennie sat down on a high stool by the table under the window and watched him. At the press of a button a large selection of possible conversation openers arose in her mind, but none of them seemed to be right for the moment. What she really wanted to ask was 'Have you changed your mind about my being here?' but she was afraid to ask in case the answer was yes. His mere presence was making her go wobbly at the edges all over again.

Then he knocked a cup over and just managed to catch it before it fell, and moments later spilled some milk, and she wondered, suddenly a light beginning to glimmer in the darkness, whether he was nervous too. As the thought came to her he turned his head and smiled again, and his eyes were shiny instead of merely flat.

'You may have noticed,' he said, 'but I'm extremely nervous. I find myself in a situation I have no precedent for.' He turned away again.

'I did notice. It was a relief. I thought I was the only one.'

'The only one what?'

'To be nervous.'

'You don't show it,' he said. 'But it's a good sign.'

'You said that before,' she said. 'Why is it a good sign?'

'Because if you were completely at ease, it would show it was all just mundane to you, a perfectly ordinary situation.'

He said that with his back turned, still fiddling with the coffee-maker, but in the silence that followed she was as aware of his eyes as if they were on her. Gulp, she thought.

'It isn't that,' she said at last.

'Nor for me,' he said. She waited until he turned round before speaking again. She thought that he would come to her, touch her, but he leaned against the unit with his hands behind him and looked searchingly into her face. His face seemed to her familiar in a way she was not accustomed to, as if it were not really separate from her. It was a strange feeling: with Miles, she had known him pretty well, well enough to know a good deal of the time what he was thinking and how he viewed things, and yet she never lost the sensation of being separate from him. While with Nick, whom she did not know at all—

'What is it you want from me?' she asked at last. He did

not answer at once, and she realised, with a sinking of her heart, that it was not because he had to think for the answer, but because he did not want to tell her.

'Don't let's ask questions like that,' he said at last. 'Let's just see what happens. Let's just enjoy ourselves while it lasts.'

The warmth drained out of her, and the feeling of unity left her. She got up from the stool in a movement which, though she didn't know it, looked weary.

'Which bedroom am I to have?' she asked. 'I'll just go along and dump my things if you'll direct me.'

He paused before answering but she didn't look at him. 'I'm in the last room on the left. You can have whichever room you like. There are two bathrooms—'

'Yes, I know. I'll use the smaller one, the one this end, then we won't get in each other's way.'

She put her bags in the room nearest the bathroom. It seemed to have been used by a teenage girl, judging by the clothes left in the wardrobe and the pin-up picture of Starsky and Hutch stuck inside the wardrobe door. It was a very old picture faded and rolled at the edges. Presumably she had outgrown them and forgotten to take down the evidence. Perhaps she had got so used to its being there she no longer saw it. That happens to people too, Jennie reflected. It had happened to Miles and her. Perhaps it was inevitable.

She did not unpack anything—she didn't think she'd be here long. She set up her portable typewriter on the dressing-table and tried it for wobble: it was adequate. She would write at night, she decided, and use the days for house-hunting.

'Here's your coffee.' Nick appeared at the door with a cup in his hand. She walked over and held out her hand for it, and for a moment she met his eyes and longed insanely to throw herself into his arms. What were they doing this far apart? But the moment extended itself and the action became impossible.

She took the cup from him and said calmly, 'Thank you. It's nice of you to let me share this place with you.'

‘That’s all right,’ he said politely. ‘It will be company. Better than an empty house.’

He might have been thousands of miles away, speaking on a telephone from Australia.

The day passed miserably. Nick sat in the drawing room and read the Sunday papers, and Jennie, who had never had time for the papers, went to her bedroom and did some work. Once into it, she never noticed the time much, and she was surprised when, aroused from her work by the sound of the front door slamming, she discovered it was after four. She was aware that she was hungry. She went out into the hall. Nick had gone out somewhere, leaving the papers spread about the drawing room; there were two empty cups and a glass on the table where he had been sitting. She had no idea where he had gone, of course. She went into the kitchen to look for food.

The fridge was well-stocked, but with such things as she felt embarrassed to touch—a whole roast duck, for instance, decorated with cherries—but after further searching she found some bread, so she set about making a cheese-on-toast: then, still being hungry, she decided to cook an omelet, livening it up with some mushrooms that looked as though they ought to be used up and some tomatoes and some Bresse Bleu and some grapes. There was some coffee left in the coffee-maker so she tipped it into a pan, reheated it, then took it back to her room and went on working.

At seven, she stopped, needing to put on the light, and found her concentration had gone. She was feeling cold and stiff from sitting in the same position all day. Her fingertips were sore from the concussion of hitting the keys, for it was a long time since she had worked for any length of time on a manual, and there was a crick in her back and a jabbing pain in one shoulder-blade from the unsuitableness of her work-desk. She knew she had better stop, that everything she wrote from now on would almost certainly have to be rewritten, but she didn’t know what else to do with herself. She was restless, bored and miserable. She had no friends in London, and the thought of going to a pub or the pictures alone depressed her.

She thought of Crete—at this time the heat would just be going out of the day and people would be gathering on their verandas for their evening cocktails and thinking about what they would have for dinner and who they would have it with. She saw in her mind's eye the colour of the sea, turning from Aegean azure to violet with the reflection of the sunset, and the texture of the hillside thrown into relief by the angle of the sun; and the first brilliant stars glowing in the turquoise sky to the east. She saw Miles in his cut-offs shuffling out in dreadful broken-down old sandals to be greeted ecstatically by Wag; she heard him telling her about his progress that day and the three-day-old news in *The Times*; she smelled the heady night scent of the aromatic shrubs and the heartbreaking smell of the sea.

What am I doing here, she wondered suddenly, *among strangers*? She was homesick, horribly homesick for a place that wasn't her home, for a husband who was no longer her husband; she was an exile in her own native land. She had lost everything; she had nothing. She sat on in the gathering darkness, too lost even to be able to cry. The telephone rang, but she did not answer it. It rang again, and for a long time, and then stopped, and as if the sound had released her she got up and went in search of whatever it was that Nick had been drinking.

She found a cupboard in the drawing room that was fairly well stocked with bottles and, not being able to find where the glasses were kept, she used the one that Nick had left out and splashed into it a generous dollop of whisky. Sipping it she went along to the bathroom and tried the water—it was hot, thank God. She ran herself a good deep bath and soaked in it for a long time, sipping the whisky, and by the time she got out to dry herself she was drunk.

A good thing too, she thought soddenly, and went back into the drawing room for some more. She left the bottle on the table in case she had to come back for a refill and took herself to her bedroom. The bed had not been made up, of course, but she didn't care. She got in between the blankets, propped herself up on the ticking-covered pillows, and sipped, and managed not to think about anything very much.

She looked at her watch when she heard the front door open again, and saw that it was half-past-ten. She listened to the footsteps, heard them stop at the drawing-room door, and imagined him taking in the half-empty whisky bottle. Inside her head she giggled. He would think he'd taken in an alky, she told herself. Then he went to the kitchen and was in there some time, though the house was too big and too solidly built for her to be able to hear what he was doing.

The footsteps came out eventually and headed towards her, and realising she had left the bedroom door open, she lay back and closed her eyes and kept still. The steps stopped at her door, she could hear him breathing, she stayed rigid, trying to breathe as if she was asleep. He stayed there for a long time, and she began to think he knew she was shamming. A desire rose in her to giggle again, and she had to pretend to turn over in her sleep to hide it. At last he drew a deep breath, which might have been a sigh, and walked on. She heard him turn the corner of the passage towards his own room, and for the next half-hour listened to him moving about, using the bathroom, padding back and forth.

Finally there was a click as he turned out the hall light, and another click as he shut his bedroom door, and then there was silence. He had gone to bed, she supposed, either to read or sleep, probably to sleep. She wondered where he had been—to see one of his other women, she supposed. Of course, it could have been anywhere—he lived in London, all his friends and acquaintances were to hand. Her own situation came again before her mind's eye, and she felt a detached pity for herself. She was sober again now, not that she had ever been more than wilfully drunk, and as the darkness and silence expanded round her, reaching out into the eternity of light, she wondered why she had feigned sleep when he came to her door.

She wanted company—why had she rejected his? It occurred to her for the first time that it might have been him phoning her earlier on. He would have thought she'd gone out. What a mess she was making of this—what a mess they were both making! He was only a few yards from her now—perhaps he was lying awake wondering where she'd been all night too. It was absurd—they were two adults, behaving like idiots. She longed to go to him. Perhaps he would come to her, as he did before? But then he had a double bed—hers was only a single. It would be better for her to go to him.

Suppose she did—suppose he was asleep? Suppose—worse—he didn't want her? He might be lying there, longing for her, but afraid to come in case she didn't want him. Impasse. She hadn't the courage to risk a rebuff. The longing to be with him, simply to be in bed with him, tucked up against his big warm body, grew and grew in her until it filled the darkness like the ache of a rotten tooth, and at last, very quietly in case he heard, she began to cry.

CHAPTER TWELVE

AFTER THE whisky and the weeping she slept late, and was roused by the telephone ringing. She struggled to wakefulness, wondering where the hell she was—she had wondered that a lot recently, since she left Crete—and as she staggered out of her bedroom in search of the phone, she glanced at her watch and discovered it was ten o'clock. Great balls of fire! The silence of the house and the fact that he hadn't emerged to answer the phone told her, when she was capable of grasping anything so significant, that Nick must have gone to work. She grabbed the phone and groped about for the number.

'Two-five-nine-one,' she said.

'Good grief, you sound gummy. What were you doing last night to make you sound like that at ten in the morning?'

'Oh, hullo, Quin.' She yawned. 'No, actually, it was whisky. I had rather a lot of whisky, and then went to bed. I was homesick, believe it or not.'

'Not, I think. At least, not if homesick means missing old Buggerlugs. Listen, if you're lonely, I'll divorce my wife and take you on, how about that?'

Jennie was forced to grin. 'I don't know what Christine would think of that.'

'Oh, she wouldn't mind—she says I'm too expensive to keep as a pet, and I scratch the furniture.'

Jennie's mind was beginning to function again. 'Just a minute,' she said, 'how did you know where to find me?'

'You may well ask.' Quin sounded offended. 'You are a bit of a pain, Savage, running off like that without telling your friends where to find you. After a great deal of putting two and two together, I swallowed my pride and my gorge and phoned old Aberdeen Angus. *He* knew, of course. What can you say about a friend who tells Count Dracula where she's going, but not her kind, lovable old buddy from way back?'

'I didn't,' she said. 'Actually, now I come to think of it, I was a bit silly. I didn't tell anyone. I expected that I would telephone people today and let them know.'

'You should have left a message at the hotel,' Quin said, seriously now. 'We might have telephoned the police.'

'I'm sorry,' she said. 'How did Angus know where I was? I suppose—'

'You suppose right. Listen, Jen, how come you fell for it?'

'Fell for it?' Jennie said flatly.

'Don't you realise you're being kept sweet? I've made some enquiries about this bloke you're shacked up with. He's been around a bit, you know—a girl in every port.'

'Yes, I do know. And about his ex-wife.'

'And they didn't warn you off him?'

'Angus warned me off him,' Jennie said, 'and Daisy. They both told me that he was dangerous, so you mustn't misjudge them. But then—'

'Yes?'

'Then he seemed to change his mind and push us together,' she said unwillingly. *It did look like it, didn't it?* 'You think he tried to put me off at first to stop me being hurt, and then decided the better way to keep me happy was to make Nick be nice to me?'

Quin paused for a long time. 'I don't want to drop anyone

in it, kid, but just be careful, eh? Use the old grey matter, and don't be taken for a ride.'

'I'm not—I mean I haven't been. We have separate bedrooms here,' she said. It was a slightly dishonest thing to say, but she could almost hear Quin's face clearing.

'Oh, that's all right then. I just wanted to put you on your guard—you know I'm very fond of you.'

'Yes, I know. Is that all you phoned for?'

'Christ no, I'd almost forgotten. I had a call from Jim Laurence this morning.'

'Oh, Jim—how is he?'

'The same. He sent his love and all things proper. One or two improper things too, which I'll tell you about another time. He wanted to know if I knew where you were, because he'd phoned the hotel in Bloomsbury and they said you weren't staying there any longer. I told him I didn't know but could find out and ring him back.'

'It must be something important for Jim to phone from Crete,' Jennie said. 'Phoning from Crete is something like trying to ski up Mount Everest.'

'Yes. He told me to give you a message, and only to phone back if I didn't manage to get it to you. He said to tell you old Buggerlugs' new hearthrob has paid him in kind. She's run off with another bloke.'

'What! Bea's left Miles?'

'So he says.'

'But they've only been together a couple of weeks. What on earth is going on?'

'It seems to be a national pastime out there, doesn't it? Jim said to tell you she'd run off with a bloke called Andrew whom he thought you'd know.'

'Andrew Lennon?'

'He didn't say a surname. Just Andrew. Do you know him?'

'Yes,' Jennie said. It was getting more incomprehensible by the minute. Bea, run off with Andrew, whom she had thought dull and boring? Andrew, soul of respectability, generally credited with a hopeless infatuation with Jennie herself, stealing Bea away from Miles? What the hell was going on out there? It sounded like episode twelve of 'Peyton Place'.

'I didn't know it could be such fun in Crete,' Quin was saying. 'I think I'll have to go over there for a holiday. It sounds more fun than ''The Archers''.'

'But surely Jim didn't phone just to say that? He could have written a letter.'

'No—he wanted me to warn you. Miles is on his way over to England, apparently to see the bods at Cavelles for something, but Jim thinks he may be trying to get you back.'

'Oh,' Jennie said. There wasn't time yet to wonder how she felt about that.

'Thing is, Jen, he's bound to contact me and ask if I know where you are. Do you want me to deny all knowledge, or tell him to bugger off, or what? Do you want to see him?'

'I don't know,' Jennie said. 'But he's bound to find me sooner or later. I'll have to tell various people where I am, and if he doesn't get it from you he'll get it from them.'

'I suppose so.'

'If he contacts you, you'd better give him my phone number. At least that way I won't get him turning up on the doorstep.'

'Okay. I'll do that. Take it easy, hen.'

'I will. Thanks for calling me, Quin.'

The phone call came sooner than she expected, at half-past-four that afternoon.

'Jennie? It's Miles.'

'Yes,' said Jennie, wondering what she felt. Dismay jockeyed with a lunatic desire to be facetious, and lost. 'It must be thousands.'

'What?'

She gave up gracefully. 'Where are you?'

'At Heathrow.' He paused for her amazement, and when it didn't come he prompted it. 'Aren't you surprised to hear from me?'

'Surprised isn't the word that springs to mind,' she said.

'Who told you?' he asked, doing some deductions of his own.

'Jim phoned Quin. I suppose you got my number from Quin, didn't you?'

'No, from Firmans, actually. It took some getting. Eventually I had to get on to Angus Mitchell's secretary.'

'She shouldn't have given you the number. How did she know who you were?'

'Well, she did. Does that mean you don't want to talk to me?'

Jennie sighed inwardly. 'It would seem churlish when you've come all this way—'

'Jennie, Bea's left me.' Jennie said nothing, and Miles spoke more urgently. 'Jennie, this coinbox is going to cut me off in a minute. Please, Jennie, can I come and see you and talk to you?'

'All right,' she said. But not here, she added mentally. She didn't want him invading this little haven, and especially she *didn't* want to be deep in the throes of a heart-to-hearter with Miles when Nick came home—if he came home. 'I'll meet you somewhere.'

'Where?' he said eagerly. She racked her brains. Heathrow was on the Pic line, wasn't it? Fear of the pips wiped her brain clean like a sponge. At last she managed to think of Russell Square.

'The British Museum. I'll meet you outside the main gate.'

'All right,' he said, too relieved at not having been cut off to object to the venue. 'I'll go straight there. I'll meet you there in—well, however long it takes to get there.'

'All right,' she said, and rang off. She was a lot nearer than him, she didn't need to leave right away; and with something of the instinct that makes a savage paint his face to frighten the enemy, she went back to her room to change into the smartest, most outrageous and most attractive of her new outfits. She felt that Miles was putting her at a disadvantage by asking to see her at all, and she wanted to redress the balance a little. He had never seen her like this before. She put on a pair of pink silk Oxford bags and a grey chiffon wrap-around blouse that tied in a knot under the bust leaving a large section of midriff bare down to the navel, and was so fine it was saved from total transparency only by some judicious embroidery over the nipples. She wore no bra under it, of course, and considering her reflection in the mirror and deciding that she'd probably be arrested if she walked the streets like that she added a pale lilac bomber-jacket decorated with the Star Fleet motif over the left breast, and finished off the ensemble with a Father Brown hat in glazed grey straw. She looked fashionable and untouchable, she decided, but if when they were indoors—in some coffee bar or restaurant perhaps—she removed the jacket, she would have all the psychological advantage that was her natural right in the circumstances.

Despite her precautions she was still at the British Museum before him, and as she walked up and down in front of the gates she began to grow nervous. She spotted Miles some way off, but so effective was her disguise that he almost walked past, only recognising her at the last minute. She didn't know whether to be pleased or annoyed at that—after all, it implied that it hadn't occurred to him that she had it in her.

'Jennie,' he said, stopping short. His awkwardness, she realised, came from not knowing how to greet her, whether to kiss her or shake hands or do nothing. What, after all, was the appropriate gesture towards a deserted wife? He was wearing a pair of very crumpled cotton trousers, a shirt with a frayed collar, and a sports jacket that she just recognised as having gone out to Crete with him when they married and never having come out of the wardrobe since. His hair needed cutting, but his suntan was magnificent, and as he looked at her with a mixture of surprised admiration and hangdog defiance he was above all familiar, and it made her heart lurch.

'Hullo, Miles. You nearly missed me then.'

'Yes—it's your clothes. You're looking very well.'

'Thank you.'

'Have you been waiting long?'

'No, not long.'

'You didn't have to come from too far away?'

'No,' she said, realising he wanted to know where she was living. His hands dangling by his side drew her attention to his lack of luggage. 'Did you come without even a suitcase?'

He looked down as if he expected to see his luggage materialise, and then laughed nervously.

'Oh, no—I have a small bag—the green check one, you know—but I left it in one of the lockers at the station.' It touched her unexpectedly to realise that of course she would know what bag he had, and that he had thought to tell her.

'Well, we can't just stand here like this. Shall we go somewhere and have a cup of coffee?'

'I'd sooner have a drink,' he said. She looked at her watch, and he added, 'Of course, silly of me, we're in England now. Licensing hours.'

It was twenty-past-five. 'They'll be open in ten minutes. We'll walk slowly to that one in Tottenham Court Road we used to go to.'

'Okay.' He fell in beside her, and they walked along in silence. It felt very strange to her to be walking like that, a few inches apart and not touching, not because they had usually touched each other when in public, but because now if they had wanted to touch it would have been difficult and possibly even significant.

'Where are you staying while you're here?' she asked for something to say.

'Cavelles have booked me into an hotel,' he said. 'Out of old habit, I suppose, they booked one near the Gloucester Road air terminal. I don't suppose anyone uses that any more. The hotels round there must have taken a terrible bashing when they opened the tube line. It's a wonder they didn't sabotage the works. It makes a heck of a difference, though, to getting into town. I could hardly believe how little time it took, and at this hour of the evening.'

She let him babble on, knowing why he was doing it. When they reached the pub the barman was just unbolting the door, and they went straight in, feeling, as the first comers in pubs always do, rather guilty.

'What will you have?' Miles asked politely.

'A Scotch, straight,' she said, knowing she was not going to get through this interview unaided. He looked faintly surprised. In Crete she had never drunk straight liquor, but then no one did out there because of the heat. Miles went up to the bar and she saw him order and then fumble around for money, and come back with his lips pursed.

'What a price,' he said in tones of injury. She sighed inwardly. He had got himself a pint of beer and now, as he sat down beside her on an imitation leather banquette, sank a third of it with a traveller's thirst.

'You're cushioned by the prices on the plane,' she said. 'You soon get used to it when you're here.' It felt horribly familiar being beside him. She felt she could have dropped her hand on to his thigh or ruffled his hair without any difficulty. It was time, she realised, to force the issue. 'And talking of that, Miles, what are you doing here?'

'Cavelles wanted to discuss the future of my series,' he said, trying and failing to look nonchalant, 'and I thought it would be a good chance to take a little break. I haven't been outside the country for—well, since we were married,' he added. Jennie looked at him steadily and waited. His expression wavered. 'She's left me. Bea's left me.'

Now you know what it feels like, was Jennie's first thought, but she didn't say it. She couldn't, even now, feel anything but affection and kindness for Miles.

'I know,' she said. 'Quin told me. He also said—' she hesitated. Suppose Quin had it wrong?'

'It was with Andrew,' Miles said, his incredulity showing in his voice. 'She used to spend a lot of time down in the village with him while I was working. At first she used to stay round the villa, but—well, she interrupted me too much. We had an argument about it—not a quarrel,' he added hastily, revealing to Jennie that they had quarrelled violently, 'and in the end I—she decided to spend the mornings helping Andrew with his shop. I can only suppose,' again the incredulity, 'that he seduced her. She sent a note up one evening saying she wasn't coming back.'

'Andrew's a very attractive man,' Jennie said gently.

'*You* never fancied him,' Miles said indignantly. 'He was in love with you for years and you didn't—and there again, if he was in love with you, what was he doing messing around with Bea? And if she was in love with me, what was she doing with him?'

His bewilderment brought back Angus's words to Jennie. He really didn't understand people at all. He had never been interested in people, so their motivations—even the fact that they might have motives for what they did—had never occurred to him. As long as they didn't cross his will, he had no need to wonder.

'You really don't understand, do you?' she said sadly.

'Well, do you?' he asked, annoyed. 'You aren't going to go all superior on me and pull that woman's intuition flannel, are you?'

'Oh, come on, Miles. Anyone who has more insight into human behaviour than you doesn't have to be flannelling, do they?'

'Well, what do you think they're playing at?' he asked. Jennie shrugged.

'I don't know. I wasn't even there. But I can think of reasons that might account for it.'

'For instance?'

'For instance—if you were swept off your feet by Bea's attractions, why shouldn't Andrew be? Nothing like her has been seen in Crete since Ariadne left for Naxos. And as for Bea—I can imagine that having been bamboozled by the legendary Miles Egerton, she found the reality a little less sympathetic than she'd expected, especially when he showed a propensity for considering his work more important than her.'

'Well, damn it, Jennie—' he began angrily. She smiled.

'Yes, of course your work is important. You would naturally think that.'

'*Any* reasonable person—'

'Perhaps that's the trouble with being married,' she went on, ignoring his interruption. 'You get so used to stepping round each other you start to do it automatically. After a while, I suppose you forget you have to try with other people, forget they might have wills and desires of their own. It can get too comfortable, especially when each of you has your own particular furrow to plough.'

'Is that how you felt?' he asked more quietly. She raised an eyebrow at him.

'It wasn't me that left you, remember,' she pointed out. He accepted the justice of that, and drank some more of his beer. She threw back the whisky and got up to go and get another. 'Do you want some more beer?'

'No,' he said absently. 'No, this'll do.'

When she came back with her drink he said, 'It seems like a kind of madness now—Bea I mean. She seemed so exciting. I felt as if I'd missed something. I felt almost—almost cheated, if you can understand that? She said she loved me. She said she was in love with me, which is different again.'

'Yes,' Jennie said. 'Well, it's always exciting at the beginning, isn't it?'

He looked suddenly into her eyes. 'Not with us. It wasn't like that with us. From the beginning, it seemed very sensible and civilised and right. I suddenly felt I'd missed out on a kind of madness I was entitled to.'

Jennie nodded. 'I know.'

'Did you feel it too, then?' he asked her eagerly. She was not prepared to answer that. She was not prepared to say anything to him about Nick, but hadn't she said to herself on meeting him that she should try trusting to instinct, rather than logic? She had chosen Miles on logical precepts, and look how that had turned out. It occurred to her at that moment that that was why she could not feel cruel towards Miles.

'I was never in love with you,' she said abruptly. 'I had a kind of esteem and affection for you. It hasn't changed. I still feel exactly the same towards you as I did before. I ought to hate you for throwing me out for Bea, but I don't. I only feel very sorry for you that it's turned out this way. I wish it had worked out for you.'

Miles blinked at that, not knowing quite how to take it. Then, manfully and blunderingly, he ploughed on.

'Jennie, if you still feel the same about me—will you come back? That's what I came here for really, to ask you to come back.'

She stared at him. 'You really are the limit, you know,' she said at last. He had the grace to colour.

'I know it must seem like—' he paused, not knowing, really, what it must seem like to anyone else. He had only considered it from his viewpoint. 'But you're a generous person. You wouldn't insist on something just for the sake of false pride. Jennie, I made a mistake—I freely admit it. I did you a great wrong, and I'm sorry. Won't you forgive me and come back? Don't let pride stand in your way. We can be happy again as we were before.'

There were so many things wrong with that speech that Jennie baulked at choosing where to start ploughing into him. While she was still speechless, he added, 'I feel the same way about you, Jennie. I realise that now. Please come back.'

Listening to him she knew it was no use trying to show him what was wrong. He would never understand. She said merely, 'I will never go back to Crete.'

It did not sound as final as she meant it to. He grasped eagerly at the straws.

'I didn't mean necessarily to Crete, Jennie. I don't know that Crete is the ideal place. It was fun while it lasted, but perhaps the time has come to move on. We could settle in the Channel Islands, if you liked. Or Ireland—we could live tax-free in Ireland.' Seeing these were still not the right answers, he added hastily, 'or even England—we wouldn't be so well off, we might even find it a bit of a pinch, but we could live in England if that's what you really want.'

'You'd be willing to live in England, for my sake?' she asked incredulously.

'I don't mind where I live, as long as it's with you,' he said. From anyone else—from Nick, for instance—it would have been a declaration of such love it would have brought tears to her eyes. From Miles it was a cry of desperation. She was to save him from whatever it was he was afraid of suffering.

'I need you, Jennie,' he said, and there was a note of sincerity in it that made her pause. To be needed—what creature didn't want to be needed? He offered her precisely the same sort of security he was, unknowingly, seeking for himself. Life had hounded him out of his den, and he found the outside world uncongenial. He wanted to get back into their warm, stinking burrow, surrounded by the reassuring scent of themselves and nothing else. He wanted her there because he was used to having her there, and because he knew she would demand nothing of him, nothing more than she had ever demanded, which demands he had got used to and could fulfil without effort.

But it was attractive in its way, wasn't it, that burrow? Here on the outside there was a cold world full of strangers. She belonged to no one, no one wanted her, no one cared if she lived or died. Well, that wasn't quite true, but there was no one who cared enough about her to make sure she was fed and healthy and happy. She was a masterless dog, and life without a master was hard and uncomfortable and demanding.

If she went back to Miles she would go back to the security of a man she knew and had affection for, whom she was licensed to kiss and touch and demand physical comfort from, whose conversation she knew and could meet, of whom she could demand with reason to know where he was and what he was doing. She would never, if she went back to him, have to walk alone in the street in a world of couples, sleep alone in a dark house, suffer the small pains and disappointments of life alone. It would be so easy to go back—much easier than not.

But something inside her revolted at the idea. Life was not for that, at least. She didn't want to suffer, any more than any other creature, but she could not accept such a bland pap of a life, not while she had the choice. She would not refuse to feel while there was feeling in her, or to fight while there was strength in her, or to hope and strive while there was life in her. The hope of something better, even with the likelihood of nothing at all, was better than the certainty of mediocrity.

'No, Miles,' she said, gently but firmly. 'When I said I'm not going back to Crete, I meant I'm not going back to you, wherever you live. I've finished that part of my life. We're going to get divorced.'

Miles looked a little taken aback, but not as much as she might have expected. He thought for a moment and then said, 'Well, you must do what you think best, of course. But look, will you come and have dinner with me, just for old time's sake? Just to be friends? I don't know anyone in London.'

She sighed, and agreed. She knew that he had not believed she meant it when she said no, and that having dinner with her was his chance to persuade her. She would have to spend the whole evening convincing him that she was not another grey cardboard cut-out in one of his books, but that she came out of a different set of novels altogether. She smiled as she sighingly agreed, knowing what an evening was ahead of her, but after all, she liked old Miles, and if it took her the rest of the night to convince him, she owed him that at least.

CHAPTER THIRTEEN

JENNIE WAS still asleep when the telephone rang the next morning, for she had not found Miles easy to convince, and when she finally parted from him she had the feeling that still he thought she might change her mind when she had punished him enough. As she went down to the phone she looked at her watch and discovered it was ten o'clock. I must have been in need of the sleep, she thought, lifting the receiver. She almost dropped it again at the sound of the familiar, dark, beautiful voice.

'Hullo. I hope I didn't disturb you?'

'I was asleep, actually.'

'Oh, I'm sorry—'

'Don't be. I should have been up. You did me a service.'

There was a pause while Nick gathered his thoughts, and Jennie repressed the desire to tell him how beautiful his voice was, and the chill it sent running down her spine. Then he said quite abruptly, 'Have lunch with me today.'

'Where?' she asked with equal economy.

'Well, I shall be at Holborn for the rest of this morning. It had better be somewhere not too far away.'

Jennie visualised Holborn, and thought of Simpsons-in-the-Strand. She had wanted to eat there ever since reading about it in a Sherlock Holmes spoof, but she had the idea it was blisteringly expensive. She was thinking again when Nick's voice interrupted her.

'Have you ever been to Simpson's?'

'No,' Jennie said, smiling to herself.

'You should—it's an experience. Do you know where it is? I'll meet you there at one o'clock. Is that all right.'

'Very much all right,' she said. Who says there's nothing in ESP?

Jennie wore her white trouser suit over a white silk blouse, thinking she had better be a little less outrageous for those hallowed portals. At the door of the shining dark place a man like the doorkeeper of a gentlemen's club stopped her with respectful firmness, and she gave him a distant, haughty smile, saying, 'I'm Mr Mitchell's guest.'

'One moment please, madam,' he said and consulted a book the size of a Bible which rested, appropriately enough, on a kind of lectern by the door. Then he beckoned to a waiter and murmured something and the waiter led her in. All very satisfyingly formal and pretentious, she thought, even down to the high average age of the staff. Nick was already at his table, and stood courteously as she was brought to him, and infected by the stateliness of the atmosphere she gave him her hand to shake before the waiter seated her.

'Would madam care for something to drink?' the waiter asked Nick, and Jennie, displaying her *savoir-faire*, addressed the reply to Nick too.

'A dry martini,' she said, and Nick translated this with a nod to the waiter who oozed away.

'A convinced feminist would have kittens,' she said, smiling at Nick and trying not to faint when he smiled back, 'but I rather like the remote-control business. It removes dining into the area of artificial insemination.'

The waiter returned with commendable promptness with a glass big enough to wash in, and waited for Jennie to try it to see if it was dry enough. It was delicious.

'At least in a place like this one doesn't have to explain that a martini is not just that stuff in the bottle,' she said, and nodded towards his glass. 'What is it you're drinking?'

'The same,' he said. That's two, she scored privately. After all the excitement the luncheon menu was rather dull, and they both chose cold soup and roast beef salad. The food at this point seemed a secondary consideration to Jennie, and she suspected, or rather hoped, to him also.

'You look very beautiful this morning,' he said when the waiters had gone. 'I don't know if you noticed, but as you walked across the restaurant all eyes were turning to you. I expect they thought you were a film star.'

'And then they saw you and were even more certain,' she smiled. He shifted his eyes.

'You aren't supposed to say things like that to me,' he said.

'Why not?'

'Because I'm the one supposed to hand out the compliments.'

'Nowadays you can't expect to keep all the good roles for yourself,' she said. She felt extraordinarily at ease with him, as if it didn't matter what she said. She studied his averted face curiously as he reached for his glass, and wondered if he were feeling the same. There was a tension about his mouth that suggested not, but when he looked back at her his wide golden eyes were shining in a way that made her feel it would take very little to put him entirely at ease.

'You were very late in last night,' he said. She opened her mouth to reply when he continued hastily, 'You don't have to tell me where you were.'

'Well, I know that,' she said drily.

'I'm sorry,' he said. 'What a very thorny lady you are.'

Now she was abashed. 'I'm sorry. Actually, I don't mind telling you. I was out with my husband. He's come over from Crete to ask me to go back to him. His affair hasn't worked out.'

Nick watched her, very obviously not asking the questions he wanted to ask. She wanted to put him on the spot, and raised her eyebrows questioningly, forcing him to comment.

'He's got a cheek, hasn't he?' he said circumspectly.

'Miles doesn't see it that way. He has a very Catholic attitude to marriage. I'm still his wife, so the obvious thing, as far as he's concerned, is to get me back.'

'I don't have any right to ask this either,' Nick began awkwardly, 'but—'

'No,' she said kindly. 'I'm not going back to him.'

'You can't forgive him?'

'It isn't a matter of that. Not even a matter of pride, really. I feel the same for him as I always felt, but I've come to realise recently that that isn't enough. I was never in love with him. I want something a little better from life.'

'So, even at the risk of having nothing at all—?'

'Oh, yes. I'll risk that—that's part of the game.'

The waiter brought their soup, and they were silent until he had served them and gone away. Then Nick said, 'I haven't seen much of you since you moved in. It wasn't for that that I asked you to share the flat.'

'I assumed that. What I didn't know was what you assumed from my moving in.'

'I just wanted you near me. I thought it would be more pleasant for you than living in an hotel, and would make it easier for us to see each other. My hours can be rather irregular. That was one of the things—' He stopped abruptly, and she gave a small sympathetic smile.

'It's all right,' she said. 'If I can mention Miles, you can surely mention Diana.'

He looked surprised. 'You really are psychic, aren't you?'

'Not at all. I'm a writer—I'm supposed always to know what's going on in people's minds in between blocks of direct speech.'

'Now you're making fun of me,' he said.

'Yes,' she said frankly, and he laughed. 'Go on, you were saying about your irregular hours.'

'That was one of the things Diana complained of. I suppose anyone in that position has the same trouble. Musicians and actors and people like that. How can you expect a partner to wait around hoping you'll come home eventually? Perhaps people like us shouldn't marry. It almost always ends in disaster.'

'The problem I think is rather that actors and musicians and people like that'—she deliberately left him out of it—'marry young, before the pattern of their lives is established, and naturally the partner resents being left more and more out of a life they were promised a share in. When such people marry later in life it can be a success. One knows what to expect by then.'

He was watching her with a smile of faint amusement. 'And I suppose a good deal depends on their choice of partner?'

'Well, naturally. If you've a life that has little room in it for anything but your work, you've got to choose somebody in a similar position, or they'll get bored. What did Diana do?'

The faint amusement deepened. 'Do? She didn't *do* anything. When we married it was assumed that a husband would keep his wife.'

Jennie shook her head sadly. 'A bad mistake that. Of course, we know better nowadays—'

'The sturdy good-sense act,' he said, smiling broadly now. 'Do you know how expressive your face is? It's like watching a play, with you taking all the parts.'

'I suppose there has to be a bit of actor in a writer,' she said, adding to herself that the important part was recognising the openings. She put down her spoon and looked straight into his eyes—not an easy thing to do. 'What do you want from me?' she asked. As she had expected, his eyes shifted away from hers as rapidly as a couple of golden snakes going to earth.

'I don't know,' he said, not sounding too happy about it. She considered.

'What about answering a few questions then?' she said at last. 'When we first met, your brother and sister did their best to warn me off you. Then when we met in Glasgow we were fairly obviously being shoved together. What was that about?'

'You found it obvious?'

'Well, didn't you?'

'Yes, but—' He didn't finish, and his eyes turned from her once again.

After waiting long enough to realise he wasn't going to reply, Jennie said, 'It was suggested to me that he persuaded you to show an interest in me to keep me sweet until I'd signed the contract.'

Now he looked at her, directly and with surprise. 'Would something like that affect your decision to sign or not sign?' he asked.

'No, of course not,' she said.

'Then there's your answer.'

'All right,' she said with a shrug. 'I'll accept that. But why did he change his mind?'

Nick evidently didn't want to answer that one. 'I suppose because he'd discovered that I was interested in you.'

'And how did he discover that?' she said remorselessly, hiding a smile.

'Because I told him?' he suggested in a small voice.

'Ah!' she said, sitting back. 'I rest my case.' He burst out laughing.

'You're wasted as a writer,' he said.

'You mean I should have been a barrister?'

'No, I mean you should have been an actress. If you had been they would still be making B films today.'

'The art of the subtle insult is not yet dead, I see,' she murmured as the waiter came to change their plates. She was happy with the warmth they generated between them, but by the time they were left alone with their salads and cold hock he had withdrawn again the few paces he had stepped forward. She let him alone for a little while, and then asked, 'Nick, why are you so afraid of me?'

'Afraid of you?' he prevaricated, and when she did not answer but continued to look at him steadily, he shrugged and said, 'You're right, of course. Well, it isn't really fear—'

'I know. But why?'

'You're so—bold, and strong. You don't seem to have any doubts about anything.'

'I have doubts about a great many things.'

'Not as many as I do,' he said. 'You seem to be able to plunge in and say to hell with consequences—'

'What else can one ever do?'

'I can't be like that. How can one ever know what's going to happen? One can't predict the future.'

'Of course not. That's why it's no use holding back.'

He looked down at his plate.

'What did you feel the first time we met?' she asked him. He shook his head. 'All right,' she went on, making it easy, 'at the very least you were interested in me.'

'You know that. Christ, you must know that—' He looked up at her then.

'There you are, you see,' she said gently. 'As long as you don't have to give it words you'll agree with it. You know what I felt then, just as I know what you felt.'

'You don't seem to find it hard,' he said. 'I can't make a commitment to you—'

'Why not?' she said. 'You have to, Nick. You want me to make a commitment to you.'

'No—'

'You do.'

'Well, yes, I suppose I do.'

'Well then.'

'But you don't find it hard,' he reverted.

She shrugged. 'I married Miles for very good, sound, intellectual, non-emotional, utterly worthless reasons. It didn't answer. Now I'm going to trust to my feelings. There comes a point when there's nothing more to be gained from holding back, when if anything at all is to happen, you have to throw caution out. It's a chance, of course, but why is that so difficult?'

'Because I can't predict what will happen—' he began, miserably and inadequately.

'Nothing will happen unless you take the brake off,' she pointed out reasonably. 'No one asks you to predict what will happen. All I ask if that you don't predict what won't happen.'

He looked up and smiled at that. 'Nicely put,' he said.

'It's my job,' she said.

'I'm sorry,' he said, comprehensively, and then looked at his watch. 'I'm also sorry that I shall have to be going soon. I wish I didn't have to—'

'It's all right,' she said. 'I have to go and see my agent, anyway. You won't be leaving me with nothing to do.'

'Good,' he said, and looked genuinely relieved. He glanced again at his watch as if for confirmation, but she recognised the gesture as a gesture of escape. He might have been a tight-rope walker looking down to see if the net was still in place. 'Look,' he began, 'I should be finished fairly early today. I could be home by about six. Of course, I don't know where you'll be then—'

She grinned. 'Very delicately put, I must say. I should be back by then, too, and in answer to the question you didn't ask, I have no plans for this evening.'

'I'm glad. Then would you allow me to plan your evening for you?'

'Provided you plan yourself into it,' she said.

She walked over to Maurice's office, rediscovering the joys of walking in the heart of London. Maurice greeted her with affection and offered her coffee.

'Well now,' he said, 'things are moving along with the right sort of momentum. You've been having a busy time recently—Miles give you trouble?'

'God, Maurice, you know everything, don't you?'

'It's my job,' he shrugged, and Jennie realised where she got it from.

'He asked me to go back to Crete with him,' she said. Maurice gave the impression of going very still.

'And are you going?'

'No.'

'Well, thank God for that,' he said, moving again ostentatiously. Maurice would have made a better actor than she would, she thought. 'You show a little bit of sense—not much, but a little bit. Going back with him would kill you off entirely—as a writer, I mean. As for the rest—'

'All right, that's the little bit of sense. What's the no-sense-at-all part?'

'You know me too well.' When Maurice smiled he could be as disarming as a shark.

'Why have you got yourself tangled up with Firman and Jackson's brother?'

'Now don't you start,' Jennie said. 'I'm a professional, Maurice. I don't let my private life influence my business life.'

'I'm glad to hear it,' Maurice said, 'because their offer came in today and I think you'll want to reject it.'

'And you thought I'd accept it simply because—'

'*They* think you'll accept it simply because.'

'How can people be so dumb?' Jennie wondered. Maurice reached forward and patted her hand.

'They don't know you, darling. They think you're some old lady with a perm and a budgie. After all, remember publishers mostly live in the nineteenth century, when women embroidered.'

'You have such a succinct way of putting things, Maurice. You should have been a writer.'

'No money in it,' he said, smiling.

'Maurice the Piranha,' Jennie said. 'He can strip a contract to the bare bones in ten seconds.'

'Talking of which, here's Firmans' letter with their offer. Read it.'

She took it from him and skimmed through it. 'No,' she said, 'I wouldn't accept that. Or that.'

'We had a busy day today,' Maurice said, reaching behind him for more paperwork. 'We had offers in from Cavelles and Mandersons too. Here.'

She read them through too. 'Maurice, am I a hot property?' she said when she'd finished.

'Until you sign the contracts, yes. Enjoy it while it lasts.'

'I can't take on both of them—I wouldn't have time. I think maybe I'd better turn down Cavelles.'

'Theirs is a good offer. You're not after Mandersons because of your friend Nick are you?'

'Maurice, I've already said I'm a professional. No, I don't think I could cope with Cavelles' series at the moment. And then again, I can always go back to them. The Manderson thing I have to do now.'

'This is true,' Maurice admitted. 'All right, I'll tell Cavelles that you're booked up for the next couple of years, but you might fit them in later. And now, if you'd like to tell me what you want from Firmans, I'll make a note and go back to them.'

One thing I want is a thing they can't give me, Jennie thought, and her expression must have shown it, for Maurice reached forward and patted her hand again, but this time more gently.

'Be careful, eh?' he said. 'I value you—don't go and get yourself too mixed up with this bloke, and get your heart broken, will you?'

'You'd get on well with him, Maurice,' Jennie said. 'He's always preaching caution too. But don't forget faint heart never won fair lady.'

'Don't forget also there's many a slip between the rolling stone and the glass houses, and that a stitch in the right place saves nine months.'

'That's positively obscene,' Jennie said.

It was such a nice day that Jennie decided to go home by bus, but she forgot to allow for the rush hour. Foreigner, she derided herself. They had no such thing on Crete. By the time she got back to the flat it was after six, and her ESP, or whatever it was that was Nick-sensitive, told her before she put the key in the lock that he was already home.

As she came through the door he appeared from the kitchen in his shirt sleeves with a tall glass in his hand and a smile of welcome on his face, and she had a sudden, painful, lovely idea what it would be like to come home to him permanently. As if he had read her thoughts he said, perhaps a little shyly, 'A bit like being married, isn't it?'

'A bit,' she said, 'although not like my marriage.'

'Not like mine either,' he said. 'Do you want a drink?'

'Yes, but there's something else I want first.' He was about to ask her what, but already she had sharpened him up. He put down the glass on the hall table and came forward and took her in his arms. The sigh that shuddered out of her was tangible as well as audible, and he held her a fraction tighter while she rested her head against his chest and smelled the scent of his skin through his shirt.

'You have the most utterly delicious smell of anyone I have ever met,' she said. He released her enough for her to look up at him.

'What sort of smell?'

'Your own smell. The smell of your skin.'

'What an animal you are,' he said, and bent his head to kiss her. It was meant, she could tell, to be a gentle, loving, salutatory kiss, but neither of them could stop, and within minutes they were clinging together like a pair of sea-anemones each trying to engulf the other. At last she dragged herself back from him, panting.

'If you intended to go out tonight, you'd better say so now, because if we go on like this, we'll never get out at all. And also, if you leave that glass there it will mark your friend's table.'

'Oh, God, yes,' he said, leaping to recover it, and dragging out a handkerchief to rub at the wet mark. 'Do you want a drink?' he asked. 'I make martinis as well as the barman at Simpson's.'

'Yes, please,' she said, thinking it was a pity how well he seemed to be able to restrain himself, especially after the way he had reacted to their kissing.

He led her into the kitchen where he had assembled the ingredients, and she was touched to see that he had put a glass all ready for her. He mixed her a martini and watched eagerly while she tasted it. It nearly blew her head off.

'Wonderful,' she gasped. 'Now what plans had you for this evening?'

'I thought I'd cook you dinner here,' he said. 'I did think

of going out, but one wastes such a lot of time getting to and from a restaurant. Of course, if you'd rather go out, you must say so—'

'No, I'm quite happy to stay here,' she said. 'What were you going to cook?'

'Secret,' he said. 'We'll start off now, though, with some paté and biscuits to stave off the pangs of hunger, because it's going to be some time before the main course is ready.'

He brought over to the table the paté and the biscuits arranged on a plate which he had evidently got ready while waiting for her to come back. Tears sprang to her eyes. It was ridiculous to find this so touching, but Miles had never in their lives together done something to please her like that. She took a gulp of her martini to hide the tears and broke into an explosion of coughing.

'Steady,' he said concernedly, thumping her back. 'Take deep breaths.' Paroxysming, she waved her hands about trying to explain to him that he was thumping the breath out of her, and then she began to laugh as well which made it worse. She gradually went scarlet and collapsed slowly and with grace on to the floor, and Nick knelt anxiously in front of her, asking her if she was all right which only made her laugh more, until finally she got breath enough to laugh aloud and he began to grin sheepishly.

'You,' he said, 'you had me worried.'

She put her arms up round his neck, and drew a shaky breath. 'Oh Nick, I do love you,' she said.

Gently he wiped the tears of laughter away from her eyes with a gesture they both remembered. 'This time I know they're tears,' he said, and then, in a very small voice. 'I love you, too, Jennie.'

She leaned forward and pressed her cheek against his. 'That's my good, brave man,' she murmured. 'It doesn't hurt, does it?'

'Not yet,' he said shakily. His arms went round her, and he drew her close. 'But if it doesn't work, it will hurt terribly.'

'Me too,' she said, 'but we have to take that chance, don't we? I love you, and I'm willing to put my money on it.'